MW01592828

THE TROUBLE WITH
PATRIOTS

Also by Tony Hays

Murder on the Twelfth Night
Murder in the Latin Quarter

THE TROUBLE WITH
PATRIOTS

A NOVEL

TONY HAYS

BRIDGE WORKS PUBLISHING COMPANY
Bridgehampton, New York

Published by Bridge Works Publishing Company, Bridgehampton, New
York, a member of the Rowman & Littlefield Publishing Group.

Distributed in the United States by National Book Network, Lanham,
Maryland. For descriptions of this and other Bridge Works books, visit the
National Book Network website at www.nbnbooks.com.

FIRST EDITION

Library of Congress Cataloging-in-Publication Data

Hays, Tony.
    The trouble with patriots : a novel / Tony Hays. — 1st ed.
        p. cm.
    ISBN 1-882593-52-9 (alk. paper)
      1. Americans—Kuwait—Fiction. 2. English teachers—Fiction. 3. Missing
persons—Fiction. 4. Kuwait—Fiction. I. Title.

PS3558.A877 T76 2001
813'.54—dc21

                                                                              2001037851

10 9 8 7 6 5 4 3 2 1

⊗ ™ The paper used in this publication meets the minimum requirements of
American National Standard for Information Sciences—Permanence of Paper
for Printed Library Materials, ANSI/NISO Z39.48–1992.
Manufactured in the United States of America.

For the real Brian O'Neill and the real Fitzy,
who were there,
and
Tom,
who knows where all the bodies are buried.

PREFACE

This is a work of fiction. The men who taught with the English Language Training Unit of the 46th Patriot Battalion, Kuwait Air Defense Brigade did so, for the most part, honorably and with that peculiar dedication found among ESL teachers the world over. It was a difficult task, and when faced with such chores, sometimes men find bizarre ways to keep from going crazy. To this much, I plead guilty.

As far as I know, however, nothing like the events described in this book actually happened. Anyone who looks to find himself here is being either highly egotistical or overly imaginative. For that matter, anyone who tries to identify me with any character within these pages is patently unkind.

Tony Hays

I dare say I may never be heard of again (I have always believed it was Ambrose Bierce's vision and not his whim that caused him to wander into oblivion). I imagine I'll have a remarkable time, wherever I end up.

—James Thurber

THE TROUBLE WITH
PATRIOTS

CHAPTER
ONE

My first glimpse of Kuwait came at twenty thousand feet and descending fast as our plane rolled out over the Gulf, making its turn inland toward the airport. "What's that?" I pointed out the window down toward a series of towers rhythmically belching fire.

"Refineries," my seatmate, a Nigerian gynecologist, explained.

"Oh, still burning from the war." It wasn't a question.

"No, no. The Kuwaitis keep them going all the time. They burn off a lot of natural gas too. They say it's easier to burn it than process it."

My first exposure to Kuwait, I thought. Wonder what the EPA or Greenpeace would say? I just nodded. Didn't quite know how to respond at that point. Settling back in my seat, I sipped the last dregs of a gin and tonic and considered my situation. Twelve months. I'd committed to twelve months of teaching English to Kuwaiti airmen. Having spent about five months doing pretty much the same thing in Japan, the idea wasn't all that alluring, but the tax-free salary offset other considerations.

I'd drifted around a lot. Got a degree in history. Tried to teach school but didn't like it. Sold life insurance. Didn't like it. Worked as a cop for a while. That was okay, but I couldn't stay settled in one place for more than a couple of years. Got married. Didn't take. As a result, I owed more people than a human has a right to, and by taking the contract, I took the one chance of paying my debts and getting free. Something about debt is emasculating, debilitating, and my ego was already pretty low. I figured two years in Kuwait and I could shed my debt once and for all. You can't make the kind of money teaching in the states that you can in the Middle East. I mean, you're looking at around thirty grand tax free to start, then add on housing, transportation.

So, given the choice between paying debts and taking bankruptcy, I'll pay debts any time. Throwing in the towel is too much like throwing in the towel. I'd never taken unemployment, food stamps, or, it seemed, the easy way out. Not that I really minded people who availed themselves of those services—each to his own; I just couldn't bring myself to do it.

So, there I was, about to land in Kuwait City, long on creditors, short on cash and motivation. One out of three ain't bad, right? Yeah, well, I guess I could learn something from Meatloaf. But the gynecologist assured me that life in Kuwait was a never-ending cycle of short work days and long wine-tasting parties. Since alcohol is illegal in Islamic society, the expatriates turn to wine as the cheapest and quickest-to-make alternative. But I'm getting ahead of myself.

We made our approach at Kuwait International Airport over the belching refinery fires and landed with a rattle and a bump, jarring my teeth and rolling the gin around in my stomach. I burped and savored the flavor of the liquor, knowing it would be at least a year before I tasted any more like it.

The gynecologist and I exchanged phone numbers, crammed into the aisle with everybody else (a situation that taught me how little is known about deodorant in the Middle East), and slowly but surely, I hit the ground in the State of Kuwait, a land even Spielberg and Lucas couldn't imagine.

The corridor down to customs and baggage claim was familiar enough, yeah, except for the policemen stationed every so often along the route. I grabbed a Pakistani skycap and waited. After a few bagless minutes, I turned to see if my help was still there. Yep, with three of his buddies smiling and scraping. I must have had "Easy Touch" tattooed on my forehead.

Customs didn't hold any surprises. A bearded officer—whose command of English seemed limited to "Open" and "Okay"—popped the top on my footlocker, checked the top drawer, noticed the copy of *Playboy* lying on top, frowned, snatched it up, and crammed it in his back pocket. My heart jumped about a foot up into my throat, but he didn't write anything down, didn't throw me on the ground and handcuff me. He just narrowed his eyes and waved me on.

I stepped through a pair of double doors and I knew I wasn't in Kansas anymore. Hell, for a minute, I thought I'd taken the space shuttle instead of a British Air flight. A flash of dizziness almost clipped my legs from under me. Arabs, as far as the eye could see. All decked out in their robes and headdresses, gray, white, cream, red and white checkered. That much seemed logical. But half of them had beepers clipped to their pockets. The other half beepers in their pockets and cellular phones glued to their ears. I caught myself checking for the Energizer bunny. It took a minute for the world to return to perspective.

"You Ed Duffy?" A remarkable voice rose from the wilderness—Boston, blue collar. I dove for the sound.

"Yeah, and it's Duffy, just Duffy. I never got used to a first name."

The man ran his hand through curly red hair and stuck the other out. "Sean Fitzgerald. Fitzy. I know the feelin'. I'm with Arthur Watson. They sent me to meet you. I was looking for a guy with enough luggage for a year and a 'Jesus H. Christ, what the hell have I gotten myself into?' look on his face." Fitzy had a way of blinking his blue eyes so that, well, they twinkled. I wanted to say it was a pleasure to be here, but "Thanks" was all that came out. He didn't seem upset at my lack of manners, but I figured that he didn't expect much from somebody flying in from London at 11 P.M.

"So this is Kuwait." I waved a hand at the cellular phone convention in front of me.

Fitzy shook his head with an infectious grin. "No. This is the airport." He pointed to the doors. "Kuwait's out there."

We slipped through the doors and I felt like somebody had shoved my head in a giant hair dryer and flipped the switch to "max." The first rush of Kuwaiti air singed my eyebrows and burned my nose. "Geez, Fitzy, is it this hot all the time?"

"Naw, it's hotter during the day."

Leaving the airport was traumatic. It represented freedom, escape, a portal back to the world. More than once over the next weeks, I'd go back to the airport and watch the planes depart with a wistful look in my eye. As my Pakistani skycap fought off the overtures of a dozen Bangladeshis trying to help, I scanned the landscape outside the terminal. Cars flashed by at the speed of light. Taxis ignored the "No Parking" signs. Nothing new here, I thought, except for the blast furnace. Could be any one of a thousand other airports across the globe. The mysterious culture of Ali Baba and his forty thieves would have to wait, it seemed, for our departure from the airport property.

Ten minutes later and we had my luggage on board a Suzuki Swift, a cross between a camel and a go-cart.

"Can't sell 'em in the states," Fitzy advised me as he cranked the engine and left a layer of rubber on the parking lot.

"Why not?" I gritted my teeth and clung to the edge of my seat.

"Don't meet the safety standards."

"Great." My excitement was barely containable.

"Just a couple of pointers. Don't look at the Kuwaiti women too hard. It's not like Saudi where you can't look at all, but the Kuwaitis get a little pissed if you throw their women more than the casual stare. They wear those veil things sometimes. Hell," Fitzy laughed. "They're supposed to make them look invisible, but all it does is draw more attention. Anyway, just avoid looking."

"Okay."

"And be careful what you say. Most of these people know enough English to figure out what you're getting at. I've seen some dumbshit make cracks about some Kuwaiti woman's ass and a few seconds later find her brother's fist in his mouth." He jammed his foot into the accelerator and swerved to avoid a Mitsubishi truck.

"Great," I repeated. Can't look at the women and can't say what you want to.

Fitzy laughed a belly-deep laugh. "Awwh, you'll get used to it. You'll get the standard orientation bullshit next week. Just think of it as a simple break in your tedium. A trip to summer camp. Why'd you sign up?" The question wasn't accusatory. Expatriates always asked each other that question.

"Money." Short, simple, and to the point. Everybody had their reasons for going overseas. Some were running from creditors; some were running from themselves. And, some, like me, needed the cash.

Fitzy nodded. "Well, if you watch yourself, you can save a bundle. Things here are pretty cheap all the way around. Your housing and utilities are covered by the company. Some guys only spend a couple of hundred a month. We eat at the officers' mess; of course, that's not contractual, but they offered, so we take advantage. Two free meals a day."

"Nothing to sneeze at," I agreed as he inserted our car between two BMWs. I glanced to either side. "Uh, Fitzy, can I ask you a question? How can the women driving those cars see through those black veils? And why are they wearing sunglasses at night?"

"It's Kuwait," he shrugged. "We'll get you a temporary driver's license in the next day or two. That'll cover you for a month, forty-five days. After that, you'll have your agama and . . ."

"I'll have my what? Iguana?" Visions of large reptiles danced in my head, and I felt the sudden pain of impending urination.

"Residence visa." Past the BMWs now, he actually used a regular lane for a change, and my heart slipped back down into place. "Uh, Fitzy, did you say you had a driver's license?" I wasn't trying to be rude, but his driving left something to be desired, like a better driver behind the wheel.

He laughed. "You'll get used to it."

It seemed there were a lot of things I had to get used to. Oh, well, I told myself. I never wanted my life to be mediocre. I stopped talking and looked out at nighttime Kuwait. Couldn't really tell much from the lights, just a mangle of highways, concrete, and square buildings. I thought about asking Fitzy if curves and circles were banned.

"What's the boss like?"

Fitzy grinned infectiously. "You'll see. Frank's supposed to meet us at the apartment complex where we live. If he remembers."

"That sounds promising."

"Awwh, Frank's okay. He's been working out here in the Middle East for ten or fifteen years. Sort of a throwback to the sixties. Spends about equal time smoking shit and popping pills. Occasionally he wanders in to work, but we send him home."

I cast a wistful eye back at the airport, now just a glow of light on the horizon. "Who's we?"

"Me and Perry Howell, the other senior instructor. See, you've got Frank, the project manager, and me and Perry, the senior instructors. All the other administration is back in Providence. Frank schmoozes them on the phone and with the fax machine, and Perry and I run the school. It don't work out too bad."

This candor, not to mention the grammar, was killing me. "How old are you, Fitzy?"

"Twenty-six."

"Why the hell are you here?"

"I was a PCV, Peace Corps volunteer, in Estonia. Got home, didn't have a job. Went to work as a temp for a congressman's reelection campaign. Then this job came up. I figured what the hell." He floored it and shot around a Rolls Royce like it was standing still, braking just in time to miss a pair of Caprice Classics that seemed intent on mating right there on the highway. "We've got some real loonies on this contract," he confided. My head just nodded. I wasn't capable of a thoughtful response.

***

The Marhaba Complex in Salmiya is a red brick building enclosed by a high wall, and the only entry is through a closely monitored, card-activated driveway. I heard that the U.S. Embassy looked at it to house employees but didn't like the security. After the bombing of the American barracks in Al-Khobar, I can understand their caution. A little sweet shop juts into the compound; trucks park there every day. Just one, with a little explosive surprise inside, and the Marhaba Complex would become the Maasalaama Complex ("Hello" becomes "Goodbye").

Anyway, Fitzy stuck his card in the slot and the arm rose jerkily. He gunned the Swift and then almost immediately slammed on the brakes. "Jesus Christ, Fitzy!" My head was doing a mamba rhythm on the windshield. I saw a tall, thin figure wearing shorts and a tee shirt, lurching into the headlights. Fitzy had almost splattered the guy across the parking lot. "Who the hell is that?"

"That's Frank. The Boss." Fitzy rolled down his window as the scarecrow staggered forward.

I cringed as a brownish-blond head of hair filled the car with a mix of Head & Shoulders, cigarette breath, and some vaguely alcoholic, yeasty smell.

"This the new one, Fitz?" His voice was indistinct, a little high-pitched, and the words slurred.

"Yeah. Frank Crawford, meet Ed Duffy. Or call him Duffy."

The figure swayed back and forth, moving from one leg to

the other looking for balance. "Duffy, Duffy, Duffy. Too much like Fitzy. We'll call him the Duffman. Welcome to fucking Kuwait, Duffman. Take tomorrow off. Hell, take the next day off too. What the fuck. Fucking Kuwaitis won't know the difference. Who's he living with, Fitz?"

"Kirby Benson."

"Is that the best we can do? I mean, the Duffman here looks like a decent guy. You got to put him with that asshole?"

I started looking back over my shoulder, estimating the distance to the airport, and wondering how far the three hundred dollars in my pocket would get me.

"Only spot we have left. We put Dougie Halpern with Jack."

"Oh, yeah, the faggot. Well, whatever. Fuck him," Frank slurred. "Fuck the Duffman too. He'll just have to live with it. Fucking Kirby Benson." And without another word, the boss staggered past the car, down the short driveway, and into the darkness.

"Is it some kind of fashion trend here to wear your shorts inside out and backwards?" I asked.

Fitzy pulled on into the parking area. "Don't mind Frank. He's just flying on hash tonight. Perry came back from a recruiting trip to Cairo yesterday and smuggled in some primo stuff. Say, how are you fixed for cake?"

"How am I fixed for cake? Sorry. I'm not much on dessert."

"No, man, cake, cash, money."

"Oh." Must be some kind of Bostonian thing. "I'm okay, I guess. I've got about three hundred dollars."

"That'll get you through a week of getting set up. Payday's not until the end of the month." He climbed out of the car and reached for his wallet. "Here's five hundred. You can catch me later."

I just stood there looking at him with five Ben Franklins in my hand. This was going to take some getting used to. "Uh, Fitzy. You don't even know me."

That completely infectious grin returned. "You've got an honest face. After we get your stuff put away, you want to go down to Pizza Hut for some chow?"

"Yeah. But, Fitzy. Is there anything I need to know about Kirby Benson? Give it to me straight."

"Well, Duff, it's like this. I used to be Benson's roommate. I knew he was an arrogant, egotistical son of a bitch. I could deal with that. Then one day, he came in and said 'Uh, Fitz, I noticed that you used a couple of sheets of toilet paper. How about kicking in five fils?' Cheap son of a bitch, too. The first night we were in-country, Frank took us to this restaurant over in Hawalli—Deek Al Roumi. All Kirby ordered was a Coke because he thought he was paying for his own. Son of a bitch was royally pissed when he found out that Frank was footing the bill."

"How much is five fils?"

"About fifteen cents. You've got a thousand fils to the dinar. A dinar's worth about $3.30. Never fluctuates much. Son of a bitch wanted me to pay fifteen cents for using a couple of sheets of his cheap toilet paper. I started to toss him out a window, but Frank stopped me. Said it'd be hard to explain to the home office."

As we talked, we moved closer and closer to Block 3 of the Marhaba Complex, the one Fitzy designated as my destination. Two young Arab kids, probably fourteen or fifteen, dressed in *dishdashas*, those robe-looking things, wandered past, giggling. Fitzy shook his head. "Jesus Christ. They've been up at Perry's, plugging him."

"Oh." There was, simply, nothing else left to say. I looked at my watch. I'd been in Kuwait a grand total of one hour, and I'd seen blindfolded women wearing sunglasses driving BMWs, a brain-burnt, opium-head project manager, and the victims of a pedophile.

Sometimes we have these epiphanies, these moments that we know are major transitions in our lives, when everything is altered. I knew, at that moment, watching those two kids walk away, that life as I knew it was over. Those dearly beloved days as a good old country boy from Tennessee were completely and irrevocably finished. I just didn't figure that the future would bring a brace of dead bodies and every major government in the civilized world down around my head.

CHAPTER
TWO

My roommate, Kirby Benson, turned out to be a little guy with a potbelly, hairy eyebrows, and an annoying habit of constantly wiping his hands on his shirt. He opened the door slowly. "What do you want?" His voice was gravelly, like he'd smoked every Marlboro in Kuwait.

"This is your new roomie, Benson," Fitzy said. "But don't worry, he suffers from chronic constipation, so he won't be using your toilet paper."

"Very funny. And why am I getting a roommate? I'm supposed to have seniority. I'm going to call Providence. They need to know how you people keep breaking the rules." Benson shot a glance at me, the eyebrows doing a credible imitation of Groucho Marx's. "No offense. This doesn't have anything to do with you."

I just nodded.

Fitzy got this look on his face, like a cross between complete, total disgust and a sudden homicidal impulse. "You can call the Pope for all I care, Benson. Just get out of the way and let this poor guy put his stuff in his room."

Benson waited. But just for a second. And then he slowly moved.

My new home beat the hell out of some dumps I'd lived in. Two bedrooms. Two full baths. Completely furnished. Living room. TV and VCR. CD player. Dining room. Buffet. Full kitchen. Microwave. I felt like I'd moved out of the trailer at last.

Kirby Benson grumbled as he pointed me toward the smaller of the two bedrooms. "Let's have some ground rules," he crackled. "Don't come in my room. Don't touch my stuff. Don't use anything that belongs to me. Don't ask me too many questions. Don't let the maids into my room. Don't let them wash the dishes. I'll wash the dishes. Don't believe anything Frank tells you about me. Don't believe anything anybody tells you about me. I like my privacy."

"Can he breathe in the same room with you?" Fitzy huffed, dragging a suitcase down the short hallway.

Kirby smirked. "I don't want any misunderstandings, that's all. I don't want no interruptions of my routine."

"Don't worry, Benson. Everybody else likes you being private pretty much, too."

I dropped my bags in the middle of the floor. "Can I ask a question? Are you people really English teachers?" It'd been my experience that English teachers were studious, scholarly, but usually professional, grammatically correct on most occasions. These people looked and sounded like escapees from a psychiatric hospital.

"I'm," Kirby pronounced pompously, "an author."

"I'm here for the cake," Fitzy chimed in.

That's what I got for asking stupid questions. So I just answered, "Okay, fine," grabbed my bags, and headed to my room.

And then the gunfire started. Not just a single shot or two, but the distinctive, rhythmic beat of an AK-47 on full automatic.

The next thing I knew, I was crouched behind the sofa while Fitzy and Benson looked at me dumbfounded. "What's with you?" Fitzy asked.

"Wasn't that gunfire?"

Fitzy shrugged. "Some Kuwaiti probably got married. They always shoot guns at weddings."

"Oh." How else could you respond to that? I opted out of the Pizza Hut excursion, and Kirby disappeared into his room, after which the sounds of fingers hitting a keyboard could be distinctly heard.

I lay awake into the early hours of the next day, wondering. But the answers didn't come, just like I knew they wouldn't. Because the world doesn't provide answers; the world only provides time, and time is a whore that we use day in and day out, and we never stop paying for her pleasures or pains.

<hr>

The next few days taught me a lot about Kuwait, especially the mosque outside my bedroom window. Muslims are prompt if nothing else. Every morning around 4:30, prayer call blasted out through loudspeakers. I also learned that two out of three inhabitants of Kuwait come from somewhere else. Only a third of the population is native Kuwaiti. There are about ten thousand Westerners in the mix out of a total of some 1.2 million expatriates. The rest are a conglomeration of Pakistanis, Bangladeshis, Filipinos, Egyptians, Syrians, and so forth and so on.

I also learned a lot about Kirby Benson. Married and divorced. One college-age son. Absolutely convinced he was a journalistic genius who had been mistreated, abused, and tormented by lesser talents. Only jealousy and envy had brought him to such low depths. Once I made the mistake of pointing out a grammar error, but he informed me that when the world realized his greatness, he could hire somebody to correct his grammar. Despite that, Kirby and I formed some kind of, well, rapport is probably the best word. Maybe accommodation. Maybe détente. No, Duffy, I stopped myself. Whatever you call the truce between us, détente was too strong a word. At any rate, grudgingly, slowly, Kirby Benson opened up to me.

About day three of my personal invasion of Kuwait, he came home from work—I was still enjoying my postarrival adjustment time—took off his shoes, and collapsed on a chair. I was watching some kind of Hindi music video on V-TV out of India. The costumes were colorful and the music had a good beat. As Kirby's weight tested the limits of the chair, a turbaned Sikh was singing Hindi rap and levitating over a big-breasted Indian woman.

"I'll tell you one thing, my boy." Kirby had quickly acquired this irritating habit of calling me that. "This shall soon be finished, 'halas' as these heathen Arabs say, over, 'c'est finis.' I will be done, finally, with this Kuwait."

Somewhere, in the back of my mind, the sentence sounded awfully familiar. But my previous attempts at conversations with Kirby had led into diatribes against every ethnic group on the globe, world hunger, world peace, AIDS, literature, and athlete's foot. "Contract about to finish?" I focused on the TV, trying to ignore the unpleasant odor rising from Kirby's feet.

"Nothing so mundane. Nothing so common." He leaned forward and looked around carefully, as if somebody were hiding behind the curtains. "I like you, my boy. I'll let you in on a little secret." Again, he checked the perimeter, the eyebrows waggling confidentially. "I'm onto the story of my life. This thing is so big it'll rewrite the history books and bring down three governments." He winked at me and grinned a jagged-toothed grin. Kirby's mouth was a dentist's dream.

Normally, I would have yawned and returned to the Hindi Top Ten, but something underlay the egotistical twinkle in his eye.

"You want to elaborate?" I asked Kirby. But even as the words came out, I saw his little roly-poly belly tighten into a great big knot. He drew back.

"Why? It's my story. I don't have to tell you. I bet you want it for yourself." He shot the words out like darts, or those little poison blowpipe arrows.

I held up both hands, palms out. "Fine. Didn't mean to intrude. And, besides, I'm just an English teacher. I'll leave the writing to you geniuses." I yawned and returned to the Hindi Top Ten.

"It's big, I'm telling you. The story of my career. Middle East policy will never be the same."

"Okay, Kirby. I believe you." I just kept looking at the girls doing remarkable acrobatics on the screen as the Sikh did a John Travolta impression while floating ten feet off the ground.

"I don't think you understand the magnitude of this. Two American administrations could fall. Two presidents could be ruined."

"Uh, Kirby. We only have one president at a time. And, besides, by the time a man becomes president, he's already ruined."

"You don't appreciate what I've uncovered."

"Enough, Kirby." I put on a very serious, adoring look. "I knew the minute I moved in that you were a brother to Woodward and Bernstein. But I also understand that these things can be delicate. Discretion is my byword."

"Maybe I'll tell you," Kirby said, slightly mollified. "You seem like a good lad. But," he sniffed. "The jury's still out." And with that he scampered off to his room, the door slammed shut, and the click of typewriter keys began anew.

The front door burst open and Fitzy fuel-injected himself into the room. The boy had more energy than four people. He was constantly in motion, constantly talking his blue-collar, Lowell, Massachusetts, jargon. "Hey, Duffy. Let's go. Off your dead ass."

"Go where?" I was comfortable.

"Up to Frank's. Big meeting. Me, you, Perry, and Frank."

"Why?" I quickly reviewed my time in-country. Nope, I hadn't broken any laws, committed any grievous sins. Mostly, I'd just watched TV and slept, with occasional side trips to the Sultan Center down by the Gulf, a cross between Wal-Mart and Kroger's. I had cussed the 4:30 A.M. prayer call every morning, but unless they had my bedroom bugged they wouldn't know about that.

Fitzy just grinned. "Can't tell you. That's for Frank. Drop your cock and grab your socks. *Yella*. Let's go!"

"Fitzy? What does '*yella*' mean?"

He looked at me like I was stupid. "It means 'let's go.'"

With the clicking of Kirby's keyboard still echoing, Fitzy and I grabbed an elevator and were whisked away to Frank's top-floor apartment.

Again, Fitzy avoided knocking or using the doorbell, and threw open the door. A bleary-eyed Frank lay prostrate on the couch. Perry, a tall guy with a hairline that receded from Washington to Phoenix, sat stiffly in a side chair, a glass of something sort of yellow in his hand.

Frank raised his head an inch. "Hey, it's the Duffman! C'mon in, Duffman!" He waved a skinny arm at a chair. "Pour him a drink, Fitz."

Perry stood and put out his hand. "Helllooo," he said in a smooth, mellow, bass voice. "I'm Perry Howell."

I shook the extended hand. No grip. It just sort of lay there, limp and unpleasant. "Nice to meet you."

Fitz jammed a glass of the same yellow stuff that Perry had into my fist. I sniffed it. Definitely alcohol or some variation thereof, but its exact composition was probably best left to toxic waste specialists. "Drink up," Fitzy urged.

"C'mon, Duffman," said Frank from the depths of his couch.

I took a tentative sip and bolts of lightning flashed across my eyes and the burn spread slowly down my throat. "What the hell is this?" I coughed.

"What a pussy! Maybe I better change my mind, guys," Frank chortled.

"It's 'E,' man, ethanol, with a little Mountain Dew on the side for flavor." Fitzy provided the commentary.

"I thought they run cars on ethanol."

"Well, they do that too. But out here we drink it."

I shrugged and took another gulp. It burned a lot less this time, and despite the motor oil aftertaste, wasn't too bad. "What are we celebrating?"

"Your promotion. Now that we're up to full staff, Providence approved another senior instructor. You're it." Frank looked ready to pass out.

And I hadn't even stepped inside a classroom. Zero experience in the Middle East. "But . . ."

Frank raised his head another inch. "But what? Who the hell else am I supposed to give it to? Kirby Benson? Shit.

Wayne Shores? Mealy-mouthed little shit. Dougie Halpern? Limp-wristed faggot.'" I saw Perry straighten his back a little. Frank caught it too. "Sorry, Perry. You're not a limp-wristed faggot. You're just a pedophile." He turned to Fitzy. "Say, what is it the boys say about Perry: 'He's not happy unless he's got one pecker in his mouth and another up his ass.'" Frank and Fitzy laughed. Perry smoldered. I took another hit of Mountain Dew and ethanol, and pondered Frank's complete dismissal of political correctness.

"I am *not* a pedophile," Perry said, addressing his comments in my direction. "I just believe that young men mature at different ages. And, like many men I know who prefer their women young, I like my men to be young, also. Is anything wrong with that?"

"What do I have to do?" Back to the subject at hand, I figured.

"Awwh," Frank said. "Don't worry about that shit now. Hell, it's the weekend. Better to get drunk and forget it all." He mumbled something else, and took another drink that mostly ended up on his shirt.

Fitzy came over and refilled my glass. "We just do the testing, assign teachers to classes, grade tests, coordinate with the Kuwaiti officers. Perry hits on the students."

"Perry Howell," Frank singsonged, "best piece of tail this side of hell."

"Don't mind them," Perry said. "They're just upset that puberty passed them by. I'd blow them, but they can't get it up." Perry stood, towering over all of us. "Now that business has been finished, I must move on. Entertaining to be done, you know. Congratulations, Duffy. I'm sure you'll do a fine job."

Fitzy slammed back his glass and killed it in about three seconds. "Damn! That stuff hits the spot." He looked at my glass.

"Drink up, man. We've got a lot of this to down. Maybe later, I'll take you over to Serge's place."

"Who's Serge?"

"Sergei Malenkov. He's the Russian consul. Lives across the hall from me. First night I moved in, somebody pounded on my door at like 3 A.M. I got up and this big bear of a guy grabs me by the hand and says come on. We went over to his apartment and shot vodka for four hours."

Disneyland. That's what Kuwait was like, I thought. Disneyland. The world's largest theme park. Only Walt Disney could come up with a place this bizarre. I glanced over at Frank, but he was passed out. His glass lay on its side on his chest, and the yellowish booze soaked his tee shirt and dripped on the floor. Fitzy was fiddling with a CD player on the other side of the room.

"What are you doing?"

"Putting on some Red Hot Chili Peppers. Ain't nobody like 'em." He grinned, hit a button, and the room was magically filled with the cacophonous sounds of my least favorite band in the world.

CHAPTER
THREE

About three hours later, I heard something like cats clawing on window screens, the noise sharp and rasping. I pried up an eyelid and looked around. Frank was snoring on the sofa, the glass still tipped over on his chest. Fitzy was passed out on the floor and the Red Hot Chili Peppers were still screeching out one of their purported songs. Seemed like the cat-clawing was a combination of Frank's snoring and the Peppers.

Trying to stagger to my feet proved to be an exercise in futility. Ethanol and Mountain Dew had done in two drinks what Jack Daniels had never done. I was completely incapacitated, immobile. I tried again, but the room was spinning faster than my head. My stomach lurched three or four times. "Show me your soul!" pleaded the Peppers. At that point they'd be lucky if they didn't see my dinner.

I heard a rustling on the floor and twisted my head enough to see Fitzy crawl to his knees. "Did we get hit by an earthquake?" I mumbled.

"No, just a quart of ethanol apiece. Frank wimped out on us. Well, come on, Duffy. The night's young." Fitzy actually made it to his feet. He staggered over and offered a hand.

"Go away." I couldn't even think about moving. A glance at my watch told me it was 1 A.M. "I'll just die right here." I closed my eyes, intent on going gently into that good night. But a not so gentle tug lifted me off the floor and set me on my feet. Fitzy was a strong boy.

"No time. Serge called an hour ago. He wants us to meet him at his place."

Seemed like with Fitzy, we were always going somewhere. I'm not sure the boy ever sat still. The room was only spinning at light speed by then, so I worked on my footing, doing a credible imitation of Frank's stagger-stepping walk, and took a deep breath. Well, Duffy, if you're going to die, you might as well go out with a bang. As we headed out the door, I prayed that Serge wasn't into the Chili Peppers.

"Fitzy!" The word exploded from beyond the door, and I watched in horror as Fitzy was engulfed by a giant bear. Huge hairy arms wrapped around Fitz, and hell, I was wondering what to tell his parents—"Dear Mr. and Mrs. Fitzgerald: Your son died in a faraway desert land smothered by a bear while drunk on gasoline. There are no remains."

"This must be Duffy!" Serge was big, six-four at least, and 110 kilograms if an ounce. Blond, shaggy hair topped his head, and a smile spread across his face. He grabbed me with one arm and crushed me against his chest, smothering my face in a shirt flavored with Aqua Velva and vodka. "Duffy! Fitzy has told me so much about you. Welcome to my home!"

Still more than unsteady on my feet, I followed the pair into a reasonably well-furnished apartment. Nothing remarkable, nothing really to distinguish it from any of the other apartments in the complex, at least none that I'd been in. Certainly nothing to identify it as the home of a diplomat. Sofas. Street Fair prints. No books. Ashtrays piled with cigarette butts. No magazines.

A bored-looking woman, about forty or forty-five, with hollow eyes set deep behind dark, puffy half-moons, sat on one couch watching me suspiciously. She was in a bathrobe and puffed slowly on a cigarette. As we took each other's measure, a girl wandered in, dressed like the older woman. But where the wrinkles ran deep in the first, the girl was an absolute, incredible knockout. Blond, blue eyes, stacked like a dozen pancakes. She joined the other woman on the sofa.

On the dining table was the least welcome sight I could imagine—a Russian smorgasbord. Pickled herring. Creamed herring. More herring than any human being should have to see at one time. Caviar. Borscht. Some kind of bizarre things rolled in little fish filets. My stomach started sending out warning signs to my mouth. But a huge arm wrapped itself around my shoulder and turned me away from disaster.

"Duffy, this is my wife, Linna, and my daughter, Marina." I judged the three. Marina was definitely her father's daughter. They shared the same open-hearted smile. The wife, Linna, forced something resembling a smirk and turned back to her cigarette. Serge completely ignored her. "Don't mind Linna, Duffy. She speaks no English. We bore her. Duffy, I want you to give Marina English lessons."

Whether from the booze or jetlag or something unnameable or unidentifiable, I started to faint. Sensory overload, I figured. Less than three weeks before, I'd been an unemployed former English teacher, former policeman, former insurance salesman, whose only hope of avoiding bankruptcy was to take a job in Kuwait. Now, after everything else I'd seen, I was being adopted by the Russian consul in a country that defied definition.

"Yeah, sure." I was more concerned with staying on my feet than Marina's education. Call me selfish. Call me rational. Call me anything. "Well, Fitz, it's getting late. Time to be going."

I headed toward the door, but Serge's hand snagged me. "Come on!" he howled. "You must to be having a drink with me. Just a little wodka. We will toast your health. And Marina's English lessons."

Fitzy was already headed to the table, his eyes gleaming at the sight of the Stolichnaya bottle. I took a leaf from Fitzy's book and concentrated on the vodka and away from the herring. "Hey, Serge," Fitzy yelled. "Duffy used to be a policeman."

Serge swiveled his big body around, the twinkle in his eye growing a little sharper. "*Walla*? You swear it?"

"What does '*walla*' mean?"

Again, Fitz gave me that 'you moron' look. "It means 'I swear' or 'you swear.'"

Okay. That made two Arabic words I understood. "Yeah. But that was a long time ago. Lot of water under the bridge."

"Come have a drink." He poured a couple of inches into a big glass, repeating the process for himself and Fitz.

I sipped, tentatively.

"*Nyet*! Not like that. Like this." Serge turned his glass up and drained it. "That is how you drink wodka."

Fitz grinned and turned his up as well. Well, I didn't have to work the next day. I could be sick all weekend. It really wasn't polite to refuse your host's request. A good southern boy would never do that. So, up went the glass and down went the vodka, moving a lot smoother down the old gullet this time. That sick, ethanol haze began to vanish, replaced by a warmer, happier vodka glow. "Hit me again," I said.

"*Walla!* He is a Russian! I swear it!" Serge grinned from ear to ear. And he filled my glass up. "*Nasdroviya!*" he shouted and kicked back another glass of vodka.

"Life is full of contradictions," I agreed, but by then I had another glassful and up and down it went again.

"So what did you do with the police, Duffy?" Serge asked.

"Just a street cop in Murfreesboro. I got on the force right out of high school. Spent a year. Went to the academy. Spent another year and then quit." I wanted to end it there. Even with the vodka working on me, I didn't want to keep talking.

"Duffy's like a jack-of-all-trades, Serge," Fitzy kicked in. "English teacher, cop, insurance salesman, army."

"Why did you stop being a policeman?" Serge just couldn't leave it.

The vodka appeared again and my glass was reloaded. "I was sitting at a red light one night about midnight, 12:30. This guy whips by me in a brand new, red Firebird, must have been doing 110. I took off in pursuit. The guy was taking corners like a master, accelerating into every curve, fishtailing and then pulling out. About five or six miles down the road, he hit a bump and tried to take out a telephone pole head-on. We found the engine sitting in what was left of his lap." I stopped.

Serge leaned forward, eager.

"Well, when I saw that it was my best friend from high school out showing off his new car, and when his father called me later for an explanation, I figured being a cop in a small town was a one-way ticket to pain. I went back to the station, and everybody was congratulating me on the pursuit, but all I could see was my buddy's crushed chest. And all I could hear was his father asking, 'Why?'"

Serge patted me on the back as Marina emerged from a bedroom, dressed in a long trenchcoat, and headed for the door. The sympathy fled from Serge's face, replaced by irritation. He shouted something guttural and Slavic.

"Out," came the response. And the door slammed behind her.

A cloud dropped over Serge's eyes, and he blinked, the cloud vanishing as quickly as it came. "We have more wodka to drink. Come, we're behind. Duffy, drink your troubles away. The only cure for sorrow is wodka." And he drained a glass. Obviously, Serge was a member of the "lead by example" club. I glanced at the closed door and wondered how well vodka salved a father's fears about his daughter.

But seconds later, another shot appeared in my hand and down it went. And the rest is lost in amnesia.

CHAPTER
FOUR

The Kuwait Air Defense Base in Subhan turned out to be a sprawling complex of low buildings, satellite dishes, and the occasional Kuwaiti in *dishdasha*. I realized that the Kuwaiti concept of a military base and the American view differed completely. A sign on the main highway at the turnoff warned "Band. Military Area." Obviously, they were in great need of English teachers.

Fitzy zipped his little Swift onto the access road, a road that seemed to dip and curve among the sand drifts, and slammed his oversized foot as hard as possible on the gas pedal. I'd finally gotten Fitzy awake at 4 A.M. to get him back to his apartment. I rolled into mine at about 4:30. I don't remember too much about the rest of the weekend. Most of it I spent with my head over the toilet. I did notice that Kirby had an unusual number of visitors, but with my self-inflicted illness, I wasn't up to entertaining.

Now I was experiencing, once more, the trials and tribulations of riding with Fitzy, as well as anticipating the pains and pleasures of beginning to teach English to the Kuwaiti Air Force. The task seemed far less daunting than riding anywhere with Fitzy, maybe because the little Swift's wheels never seemed to touch the pavement; maybe because Fitzy was completely and totally oblivious to the brake pedal.

He did slow down somewhat as we approached what appeared to be a main gate. Two guards were kicked back in their chairs, their M-16s lying aimlessly (no pun intended) across their laps. One raised his beret and, seeing Fitzy, waved and dropped the cap back over his eyes. The other didn't bother to wake up.

"Really on their toes, aren't they?" I mean, here we were in the land of Mohammed and a thousand shrieking terrorists, and the guards at the Air Defense Brigade couldn't even wake up long enough to check our IDs. Not that I had one, of course, but the gesture would have given me comfort.

"Awwh, they know me. Besides, why would anybody wanna blow up this place?"

He was right. The base looked like a ghost town. Weeds grew in the cracks on the sidewalks. Trash—candy bar wrappers, cigarette butts, soft drink cans—lay piled up against the curb. The paint on the massive "Air Defense Brigade" sign had worn so thin that it seemed to read " ir De nse B ad " which sounded like bad German.

"What about Saddam Hussein? Don't they worry about another invasion?"

Fitzy shrugged. "Why? The 5th Fleet is out in the Gulf; there's a couple of thousand U.S. troops up at Camp Doha. Son of a bitch wouldn't last ten minutes."

"Then why are we teaching these guys how to fire Patriot missiles?"

"Payback. Ninety percent of defense contracts handed out by the Kuwaitis since the war have gone to the U.S. and England. Payback. It's as simple as that. Besides, the Kuwaitis are staffing the battalion with triple redundancy. For every one American assigned to a specific job, the Kuwaitis assign three."

"Why?"

"To make sure that at least one of them is there to push the button at the appropriate time. Besides, they don't worry about money the way Congress does."

Okay. I could buy that. I mean, if there was anything Kuwait had plenty of, it was money. Fitzy hit a roundabout at about sixty kilometers an hour, fishtailing a little and just barely missing two little fellows in desert camouflage. "Who are they?"

"Bangladeshi. The Kuwait government hires thousands of them. They stand guard, dig foxholes, get tea for us. It's a pretty sweet deal for the Bangladeshis."

"How do you figure?"

"When they get over here, they've got nothing except the clothes on their backs. The Kuwaitis give them uniforms, equipment, rifles. When their time is up, they go back to Bangladesh with everything."

"So, in essence, Kuwait equips the Bangladeshi army?"

"Yeah," Fitzy confirmed, "that pretty much sums it up."

I kept my own counsel for a few minutes until Fitzy slid to a stop behind a group of two-story buildings set back away from the rest. A sign was tacked up over a door—"46th Patriot Battalion." About a dozen men in blue uniforms loitered around the doors, smoking cigarettes and holding hands.

"Fitzy, why are these guys holding hands?" I waited for the answer before I got out of the car.

Fitzy just laughed. "Awwh, man, they do that over here. It's no big deal."

"Do you let them hold your hand?"

"Hell, no! First son of a bitch that tries is history."

I was relieved. A few other cars started rolling out and I saw my roommate, Kirby Benson, climb out of one.

"Has Kirby been like this ever since he got here, or did he become paranoid-schizophrenic in-country?"

"Naw, he's always been like this. Frank found out that he got fired from his last job down in the Kingdom because he started investigating the *mutawas*."

"Where's the 'Kingdom,' and what the hell are *mutawas*?"

"Saudi Arabia. Everybody calls it the 'Kingdom.' *Mutawas*? They're like religious policemen, the guys you see in the high-water *dishdashas* and long, scraggly beards. Real fundamentalists. Here, they just stomp around and look like wackos. Down in the Kingdom, they're like semiofficial, and they go around with these little sticks and hit people that don't follow all the rules."

"Charming." But the explanation made me wonder about Kirby again.

"*Yella*, Duffy," Fitzy shouted. "Let's go. Today's the first day of a new cycle. We're on a two-week POI—that's program of instruction. We teach them the Defense Language Institute curriculum. It's a set of thirty-six books in the most God-awful, boring methodology ever invented. You'll fall asleep trying to teach it. You're lucky, though."

"How's that?"

"Since Frank upped you to SI, you'll only be substituting as necessary. Let me tell you. When you're teaching this shit five hours a day, you go crazy."

"What are the students like?"

Fitzy just grinned. "That you'll see for yourself."

We kept walking between grinning, uniformed Kuwaitis remarkably unlike the other citizens I'd become used to back in town. These guys looked, I don't know, rougher around the edges despite the uniforms, and they were young—seventeen, eighteen. A pair of eucalyptus trees shaded an interior court-yard and the guys gathered in little groups of two or three, chain-smoking and holding hands, occasionally pecking each other on the cheek as some newcomer joined the circle.

Inside the building was as complete a replica of an American military complex as I'd ever seen, right down to that General Services Administration smell on the desks and chairs. They must import it in spray cans. Probably, some little Bangladeshi's main job every morning is to give everything a quick squirt from a can marked "Odor, U.S. military, boring, but distinctive."

Fitzy guided me into a long office littered with desks topped with large blue paperbacks, their covers reading uniformly "American Language Course," with varying book numbers. A half-dozen Americans stood at the back of the room hovering over a whistling kettle. Perry Howell breezed into the room and sat down opposite another instructor, a young, bespecta-cled guy with peroxide blond hair. Within seconds they were head-to-head.

Fitzy pointed me toward an empty desk in one corner, as he casually glanced back toward the pair. "That's Dougie Halpern. He and Perry are probably talking about the guys they blew over the weekend. It's like a contest between them to see who can give the most blowjobs in a forty-eight-hour period."

"Yeah, okay, but they keep looking over here at me."

"Don't worry. They're probably just seeing if you stand to be any kind of competition."

Fitzy pointed to a desk. "That's yours. But most of the time, you'll be across the hall in the main office. That's where me and Perry hang out. Frank uses it too, when he shows up."

"Will Frank be here today?" I needed to get reimbursed for some shipping receipts.

Fitzy grinned. "Officially," he said with a wink, "Frank has strep throat."

"How long will he be out?"

"Until the case of ethanol that Perry got him runs out, not to mention the hash that Perry brought back from Cairo."

—◆—

"Fitzy, I'm sick and tired of the schedule changing every stinking day!" An old guy, mostly bald with a white fringe circling his skull, stormed across the room waving a piece of paper. I noticed a globe and anchor tattooed on his forearm.

"Jesus, Jack. I can't help it if the Kuwaitis keep changing their fucking minds! Okay?"

"Well, somebody needs to show some balls around here and get this straight. Every goddamned day it's something different. I don't know how you expect me to teach with all these changes . . ." and Jack wandered off, huffing and puffing.

"Fucking faggots," Fitzy muttered.

"What? The guy's an ex-marine."

"Yeah, right. You know how many ex-marines are gay? Too damned many."

"Goddamnit Fitzy!" An all-too-familiar voice exploded across the room, and I turned to see Kirby Benson advancing on us at full steam waving his eyebrows and a piece of paper identical to the one held by the effervescent former marine. "I told you I didn't want these guys anymore. All Mohammed Awad can talk about is his stinking camel! I can't get these guys motivated to study English. They can't even speak proper Arabic."

"Do you speak Arabic?" I couldn't help asking.

"Well, no." My question stopped him in his tracks.

"Then," I said in a more even tone, moving forward and putting my hand on his shoulder. "I suggest that you concentrate on new ways to get these guys moving. Look, Kirby, Fitzy gave these guys back to you because you're the only one who can handle them; you're the only one they respond to."

"Really?" Kirby was entranced by the idea.

"Absolutely. Why just this morning, Fitzy was saying that he wished he had twenty Kirby Bensons. Your experience and personality in the classroom combine to make you an especially potent force. We need you on this one, Kirby. You're the only one who can handle these boys. We're depending on you, Kirby. You can't let us down."

"Well," said a suddenly humble, quieter Kirby Benson, "I just try to do my best."

"And your best is incredible. We need you, Kirby."

"If you think I'm the best suited," he mumbled.

"Unquestionably." I patted him on the back.

"Okay, then." And Kirby Benson wandered off, eyebrows still, in contemplation of how to handle whatever group of hellions Fitzy had saddled him with.

"That," Fitzy began, "was more than incredible. That was artistry in motion. You're going to fit in just fine around here." He turned to the gathering, now some twenty-odd strong. "Hey guys!"

All heads turned in his direction.

"This is Ed Duffy, a newby on the scene. Because of his great credentials, Frank has named him as the new senior instructor effective immediately. He's from somewhere in the South; you'll like him."

Heads nodded at me. The response was generally favorable, but I did see a couple of silent, belligerent stares. I noted the faces for later. Just in case.

Fitzy jammed a piece of paper in my hand.

"What's this?"

"Your orientation schedule. Home office requires it. It's basically a jerk-off session, but you ought to get a laugh or two."

~ ~

Fifteen minutes later, I was still waiting for the laughs. Kirby Benson had just completed a particularly dry recitation on the Defense Language Institute curriculum, filled with references to acronyms like MLI, ECL, ALCPT, POI, USAMC, OMCK, and a dozen others I didn't bother to write down. The gist of it seemed to be that rote memorization was the basis for the DLI method, despite the fact that nobody had used it as a teaching technique in the last thirty years.

Kirby closed his file with a smart-ass smile. "That ends my briefing. And now, my boy, I'll turn the floor over to Mr. Howell, who will give you your cultural orientation."

Perry approached the lectern and placed a stack of three-by-five cards before him. "Good morning, gentlemen." I looked around, but besides Fitzy and Kirby, I was the only one in the room. "I have been given the task of providing you with some cultural background on this exotic land."

Fitzy rolled his eyes.

Perry turned and wrote three letters on the white board. "I. B. M."

"Excuse me." There had to be something more productive to do than watch a pedophile practice his ABCs. "What does IBM have to do with Kuwaiti culture?"

Perry pulled his wire-rimmed glasses down over his nose like a professor. "Please hold all questions until afterwards." Duly chastised, I folded my hands and contemplated wrapping them around Perry's throat.

"The entire Arab world evolves around this concept. It is the glue that binds society. It is the concrete that hold the structure in place. It is the—"

"C'mon, Perry," Fitzy exploded. "Just get on with it."

I flashed Fitzy a look of gratitude; Perry tossed some retinal daggers.

"*Inshallah, boukara, maalesh*," he intoned. "Please, repeat after me."

"You've got to be kidding."

"Do I look like I'm kidding?"

"Perry!"

But Perry smiled a perverted little smile. "It's my orientation."

I threw up my hands. "*Inshallah, boukara, maalesh.*"

"One more time," he commanded. And I complied, feeling like an absolute dolt.

"Now, professor, what the hell do *inshallah, boukara, maalesh* mean?"

"'God willing, tomorrow, never mind.'"

"And that's the concrete that binds this society together? Sounds like a litany of excuses for things that never get done."

Perry jerked his head back like I'd pasted him one—something that sounded like a lot of fun—and pushed his glasses back to their proper position. "Oh, my God! They've sent us one with a brain!"

For no discernible reason, I felt a certain pride in having Perry consider me intelligent. "Thank you," I said. "I'll sign autographs later."

"Good answer. Now, you'll hear those three words uttered a hundred times a day in response to even the most basic query, such as 'Will my clothes be finished soon?' *'Inshallah, boukara'* will be the reply, even if they don't have the slightest idea when your clothes will be finished.

"The other guiding principle of this society is *wasta*, or 'vitamin W' as it is better known."

I raised my hand dutifully.

"Yes?"

"What exactly is *wasta*?"

"Loosely translated, it means 'influence.'"

"So? Every society has influence."

"Yes, but the Arabs have institutionalized it. What you get and how quickly you get it are directly related to how much *wasta* you have. Come here," he said, heading for the window. He pointed at a jeep parked across the lot in front of battalion headquarters. A sergeant sat in the driver's seat.

"Okay. Now, what?"

"Wait for it."

A couple of seconds passed and then an incredibly overweight private came out, climbed in the jeep, pointed a direction and off they went.

"So?"

"How many privates in the U.S. Air Force have sergeants for drivers?

"I see your point."

"Now, Kuwait claims to be a constitutional monarchy, but only if you use a loose definition. Actually, Kuwait is a cross between a totalitarian dictatorship and a hereditary monarchy, with a manic-depressive kindergarten parliament thrown in for appearance's sake. Sheikh Jaber al Ahmed al Sabah is the emir. He is lovingly referred to by his people as 'Baba Jaber' or 'Father Jaber.'"

"Sweet."

"Appropriate," Perry retorted. "At last count, Sheikh Jaber had 168 children by an unknown number of wives."

"Busy man."

"He actually looks a little tired these days," Perry answered sadly. "Now, if you are pulled over by Kuwaiti policemen, smile and flash your passport. They typically can't read, but they recognize an American passport when they see it. Being an American has its privileges. Conversely, if you have a car wreck with a Kuwaiti, you may as well kiss your proverbial ass goodbye. This is a class system, and Westerners rank behind Kuwaitis. But it's not all bad. We rank ahead of Egyptians, Yemenis, Palestinians, Indians, Pakistanis, Sri Lankans, and Filipinos."

"Comforting."

"Quite. Booze can be bought on the black market for about $120 a bottle. . . ." Perry droned on with other practical tips. I had to give him one thing; he was at the very least more informative than Fitzy. But then Fitzy had been practicing his driving skills on the Kuwaiti National Speedway and wasn't giving me his full attention.

"You will notice," my lecturer continued, "that many of our colleagues are gay. While the Middle East doesn't cultivate this type of behavior, it is sympathetic to it. Since Arab males and females aren't allowed to consort sexually until marriage, many males burn up all those frustrated hormones on Western gays. You see, they don't consider themselves homosexual, rather it's the one they're doing it to who is gay. In an effort to remain sensitive to their feelings, please refrain from referring to your gay colleagues as 'flamers' or 'faggots.' However," he said with a disapproving sniff, "the terms 'fairy' and 'queer as a three-dollar bill' are allowed.

"Finally, never, ever, for any reason, drive in the desert on anything other than a well-traveled road."

"Why not?"

Perry smiled wickedly. "Four million landmines left over from the war." He looked at his watch. "Oops! How time flies when you're bored. I have a previous engagement." Without another word, he disappeared out the door. I looked at Fitzy, my head spinning from the Perry Howell Show, and he shrugged.

"To understand Perry," Fitzy explained, "is to know him. I'd rather stay ignorant."

Now I knew why I'd been hired. They'd take anybody.

A few minutes later, I was easing down at my desk in the teacher's room, thinking the worst was over.

"*Salaam aleichem*," a voice from the door greeted.

"*Aleichem salaam*," came the thunderous reply from the teachers.

I turned and saw a short man, thin, with a pencil mustache, dressed in the blue of the Kuwait Air Force. On his shoulders were small, crown-shaped, gold insignia.

"Guys," he said to Fitzy and Perry. "Can I see you for a minute?"

They immediately turned to follow him. Fitzy gave me a "c'mon with us" look, and I trailed along.

Across the hall, we entered a small narrow office manned by a short Indian with a painted-on smile. Fitzy nodded to him. "That's George. He's from Goa or Calcutta or Delhi or somewhere. He keeps track of everything." George's entire career was summed up in three sentences.

We moved into the next room, a big one with a large conference table close to the left wall. Photos of Patriot missiles in action decorated the walls, and a huge American flag hung above a giant blackboard. The Kuwaiti officer sank into a big swivel chair.

"What's up, Major?" Fitzy broke the ice.

"Guys, we've got a big problem. The heat's on to graduate more trainees," the major said, his eyes flitting around. "Where's Frank? I was hoping he'd be here."

"Frank has strep throat," Perry said quickly. "He'll probably be out for the better part of the week."

The major eyed him carefully, started to speak, and then didn't. After more than an awkward pause, he finally spoke through tight lips. "Guys, you're going to lose this contract if you don't get more people through the program. That's the bottom line."

CHAPTER
FIVE

"But, Nasser," Perry began. "You know what we have to work with. These boys just aren't teachable. I mean c'mon, puh-leeze!"

Major Nasser chuckled a little. "Guys, I know what you're saying. But I also know what headquarters is saying. And Colonel Jassim is not happy." He paused and looked at me for a second, a quizzical look clouding his face. "Do I know you?"

"Sorry, Major," Fitzy slid in with the introductions. "This is Ed Duffy. Just call him Duffy. He's the new senior instructor. You'll like him; he's a good guy."

With the Fitzy seal of approval firmly affixed, I put my hand out and Nasser closed his around it, firmly. "Your English is excellent, Major. Did you study in the states?"

Nasser smiled. "In a manner of speaking. I was with the Hawk Missile Battalion some years ago, and I trained at Fort Bliss, Texas. I'm sure that didn't hurt my English, but that's not where I learned most of the language."

"Where then?"

"Well, Duffy, I learned English with my American girlfriend in El Paso and Spanish from my Mexican girlfriend down in Juarez. The bed is the best possible classroom."

I couldn't help but laugh. Major Nasser was a small man, he carried himself with confidence, and his English *was* impeccable regardless of where he learned it.

"Look, I'm on your side, guys. Okay? But I've got people upstairs to answer to. You've got to figure out a way to get more of these boys through here and shipped over to Fort Bliss. If you don't, you can kiss this contract goodbye." He stood to leave but paused for just a second. "Tell Frank that I hope he feels better."

"Well, fellows, this is what I call job security." I'd been in-country less than a week, and I was already looking at the possibility of unemployment.

Fitzy cast a look at Perry. "I've never heard Nasser that blunt before."

Perry nodded. "I don't know about you fellows, but I enjoy the lifestyle I lead. If this doesn't get fixed soon, we might all be looking for jobs."

"Hell, Perry, you could go back to the Emirates," Fitzy chuckled.

"And get stoned out of my apartment again? No thanks."

"Stoned out of your apartment?" I was intrigued.

"Never mind."

"We could fiddle with the book tests," Fitzy offered.

"What's a book test?" Most of Perry's orientation spiel had been lost on me.

"At the end of each two-week program of instruction, we test the guys in the book they've been taking. If they hit 70 percent, they move on to the next level. Anything below and they repeat the book," Fitzy explained. "Our failure rate is about 60 percent."

"Yeah, and sometimes higher." Perry said, his tone slow and modulated. "We could do that, but that doesn't solve the problem of the English Comprehension Level test. We can't screw around with that. The U.S. Embassy boys administer that one. The guys have to score at least 50 to go to the states. We don't have any control or access to the ECLs."

Something about this picture bothered me. Here we were, three supposed administrators on a U.S. government contract, and we were openly discussing fraud as an acceptable means of keeping our jobs.

"Why don't we call Frank?" I suggested innocently.

"Naw," Fitzy said. "That'll just make matters worse. Frank'll show up higher than a kite, and that'll just convince the Kuwaitis to cancel the contract."

Perry nodded in agreement. "Well, I have work to do. You two figure something out."

So Fitzy and I were left alone. "What should I do?"

Fitzy shrugged. "I don't know. I'm going to do the crossword puzzle. Why don't you play solitaire on the computer or something?"

"Aren't there, like, administrative things to be done?"

"Naw, George takes care of all that. I mean if something happens, like a trainee pointing his rifle at one of the instructors, we'd take care of it. But otherwise, nope. Concentrate on solitaire."

"What's Perry doing?"

"Who knows? He could be plotting which teaboy to hit on next. He could be working on supplemental material for one of the teachers. With Perry, you can never tell."

"Shouldn't I be doing something like that?"

"Geez, Louise, man! Quit being such an eager beaver. Just play solitaire and let your feet get wet little by little."

So, I spent my first day earning a whopping, tax-free $30,000 a year by playing solitaire. The occasional Kuwaiti wandered in, but either George handled it in a mishmash of English and Arabic, or Fitzy stomped over to Major Nasser's office and resolved it. My efforts were not required.

At home that night, Kirby stayed bottled up in his room. About 9 P.M. the doorbell started ringing.

I answered the door and a bearded Kuwaiti in *dishdasha* stood there looking imperious.

"I must see Mr. Kirby."

I let him in and he padded down the hallway to Kirby's room. "Kirby," I yelled. "Somebody's here to see you."

The door slammed open and Kirby's uncombed head popped out. "Who is it?" He squinted at the Kuwaiti. "Yeah, right. C'mon back, Abdulmohsen."

The Kuwaiti disappeared into Kirby's room and Kirby, slicking back his hair with one hand, glared at me. "He's not here. You didn't see him. You've never seen him."

I returned to television. An hour later, the doorbell rang again, but before I could make it to the door, Kirby bounded out, the Kuwaiti in tow, and dashed into the kitchen, shouting back at me, "Don't let them in until I get Abdulmohsen out of here." So I stood there looking remarkably ineffective while Kirby shuffled his visitor out the back door.

In seconds, he reappeared. "Okay. Let him in."

I opened the door with a snarl running across my face. What the hell was Kirby doing? "Yeah, can I help you?" I asked without looking, and another *dishdashaed* man bolted into the apartment.

"Where is Mr. Kirby?" That was all. Not even a "Hi, how are you?"

Returning to the television, I watched an old *L.A. Law* episode, trying to forget my roommate and his visitors. But that only lasted another hour, at the end of which Kirby trundled out of his room alone.

"Somebody else will be here in a minute. Send him straight back."

"Do I look like your receptionist, Kirby?"

Right on schedule, the doorbell rang. "Kirby Benson's office, may I help you?" I chimed pulling the door open. But, instead of the Kuwaiti I expected to see, I was confronted with a Bangladeshi wearing soiled, orange coveralls.

The little man's eyes flitted about nervously. "Where Mr. Kirby?"

Two Kuwaitis and a Bangladeshi; it didn't even sound like a good poker hand. Whatever Kirby was up to, I didn't want anything to do with it. I sent him down the hall as I checked my watch: 10 P.M. Too early to go to bed, too late to stay up.

Relaxing on the couch, I tried to figure the day out. Supposedly working on a respectable government contract, instead I was participating in discussions about fixing test scores, telling lies to cover an alcoholic boss, and acting as doorman for my roommate. Jetlag was a piece of cake. So, I opted to head down to the Sultan Center and pick up some groceries. Couldn't be crowded at 10 P.M. Just goes to show how little I understood about Kuwait.

The Sultan Center was ten deep in every aisle. Looked like a Blue Light Special at K-Mart. I dodged little Kuwaiti kids with my cart, barely avoided taking out a trio of Pakistanis who were marveling at the Charmin toilet tissue, and finally dashed into the cat food aisle.

And slammed right into a brunette with a mean look on her face.

Groceries went flying—I personally witnessed a jar of Beluga caviar collide with a can of Whiskas cat food.

"Sorry about that," I muttered.

The brunette paused for a second. "You're American."

"That's what my parents told me, not to mention my passport."

Her expression softened. "Sorry, I was prepared for the typical Arab assault, or the Pakistani protestations 'I didn't do it.'"

"Been here a while," I noted, retrieving a box of Cheerios from the floor. The brunette was kind of pretty; you know, the kind who's hard to judge at midnight when no previous attempt has been made at freshening up. Her nose was slightly off center, but her hair tumbled down over her shoulders.

"Is there something wrong?"

I was squatting there staring at her with a jar of Vlasic pickles in my hand. Hurriedly, I stowed the pickles away and searched for a botched answer—realizing in advance that it would be botched.

"No, I've just always admired the Vlasic packaging strategy."

I got a sour look for my lame effort. "That has to be the worst line I've ever heard in my life."

"What do you expect at," I checked my watch, "midnight?"

"Granted," she nodded. "Karen Solomon." She produced a soft, slightly tanned hand.

"Ed Duffy. Confidentially, does everyone here have their times screwed up or are they all just vampires who shop at midnight?"

That one produced a genuine laugh. "Meteorological. Too damned hot to shop during the day."

"Good point. Listen," retreating back to my tried, true, and obvious lines, "now that I've assaulted your groceries, can I buy you a cup of coffee?"

"Don't drink coffee," she began, and, of course, my face fell about four feet. "But, I'd love a Perrier."

At any other hour, my remarkably bad record with women would have appeared in neon floating above the Calvin Klein display, but, true to form, I smiled as wide a smile as my flesh allowed and said, "I'm sure that's on the menu." We adjourned to the coffee shop upstairs after parking our carts beside the escalators. The place was crammed with *dishdashas*—sort of looked like a marshmallow convention—and black-veiled women with mobile phones pressed to their ears. Smoke hung vaguely like a purplish blanket over the entire room. A chipper-looking Filipino hostess bounced up and said, "Smoking or nonsmoking?"

We were led through this, I don't know, gauntlet—men on one side, covered and veiled women on the other. Little white pieces of paper kept flying across the aisle, an assault that both Karen and the hostess ignored. I felt like I was back at a Vanderbilt basketball game as the fans expressed their displeasure at a ref's call, but I observed in silence until we were seated by the big picture window.

The Arabian Gulf is beautiful, especially at night, especially in Kuwait. The lights of the city reflected whitely off its darkened waters, the commanding figure of the giant, turquoise Kuwait towers looming along the coast further toward the city. It would be wrong to call Kuwait a fairyland kind of world, but even after the Gulf War, the wealth, the opulence were still evident.

"So, Mr. Ed Duffy, when you're not assaulting helpless shoppers, what else do you do?"

"Listen," I began. "I *am* sorry about ramming your cart."

"I just thought you were getting in practice for old age."

"How's that?"

"Well, out in the American suburbs, these old men cruise the aisles with grocery carts intent on slamming them into the first good-looking woman they see." She grinned as she said it, with the corners of her mouth turning up just the slightest bit, just enough to show she didn't disapprove of the old men in question.

"Nope, I've never been that forward. I was one of those guys in college who sat across from the sorority chapter rooms on Sunday night and drooled as the girls filed in."

I tend to fall in love about fifteen times a day. That was my problem. And with Karen Solomon, it took me all of about ten minutes to become completely captivated. Without being too obvious, I checked for the expected wedding band. My attempt was as successful as usual.

Karen held her hand up for inspection. "Nope, no rings."

"Sorry."

Karen just laughed. "Why should you be? It's a natural reaction around here. So is there a Mrs. Ed Duffy?"

"Used to be, but she objected to my lack of organization and disinterest in having a steady job."

"Okay, fair enough," she agreed, after the waitress brought my coffee and her Perrier. "But wasn't there anything *you* objected to?"

"Yeah," I said after a few seconds. "I objected to her agenda for me. She's one of those crusaders; you know, the kind that marries a bum intending to change him, to make him the man she wants him to be. Well, unfortunately for our marriage, I'm genetically incapable of changing, some kind of mismatched chromosome."

"In other words, she gave up on you?"

I laughed. "More or less. What about you? Was there a Mr. Karen?"

"Yeah. But he was in the foreign service too, and our careers took different paths. I was an Arabist and he specialized in Eastern Europe. Not too many posts in Eastern Europe call for Arabists."

"Nor," I answered, "would I think there would be too many Arab postings that require Eastern European specialists."

"More than you might think."

"Yeah?"

"All these posts out here have Russians assigned to them. Knowing what those boys are up to is just as important now as it has been for the last seventy years or so."

"Most of them—at least the ones I know—are busy drinking themselves to death."

"You know Russian diplomats?" She obviously couldn't believe her ears. And for some reason, I was offended.

"Why not? I'm a reasonably well-educated man, a decent conversationalist, and generally a nice guy."

"Agreed," Karen nodded. "So what do you have in common with them?"

"Nice recovery," I granted with a bogus nod.

"I'm a diplomat. Specializing in nice recoveries was my major in diplomat school."

"Doesn't that imply that our diplomats commit too many faux pas?"

"Granted. But, just in case you were curious, some of the faux pas we handle are created not by diplomatic types but by well-meaning American citizens who for any number of reasons step on it in foreign lands." A little crust covered her voice.

"Yes, stupidity is an illness common among our people," I agreed pompously, and stupidly, I thought, but that just proved the point.

She smiled, breaking the crust a little, and I zoomed back in from the stratosphere. "Stop it; you sound like Walter Cronkite."

"Sounding like the former most trusted man in America is also an illness common among us."

"Former?"

I leaned across the table conspiratorily, as if I were passing some deep state secrets. "Don't look around. And don't be surprised, but you have to be past thirty to remember Walter anymore. He retired like fifteen or sixteen years ago. Today's younger generation has no idea who Walter is or was and couldn't care less. To them, the most trusted man in America is the artist formerly known as Prince."

"Okay," she admitted begrudgingly. "So I've seen the better side of thirty. You're no spring chicken."

"I'm edging over into the grave, lady. I hit forty this year. And that's a frightening thought for the little boy who never grew up."

Just about then another barrage of white flew through the air from one row of booths to another across the aisle. I couldn't stop the confusion wrinkling my face. "What the hell?" I also couldn't keep my mouth shut.

Karen swiveled. "You mean the occasional blizzard?"

"Yeah. What is that?"

"Simple. Being Arabs, boys and girls can't sit in the same booth and flirt. They must resort to subterfuge, clandestine actions. So, they sit on opposite sides of the aisle at Jean's Grill and toss their mobile phone numbers to each other so they can chat in the privacy of cyberspace."

"You're not serious?"

"Completely. They're allowed virtually no public interaction, so they revert to modern technology to get around cultural and religious barriers. I've been out here for a year, and it's taken me that long to figure some of these things out."

"I bow to the voice of experience." Checking my watch, I saw that one-thirty was approaching, and about four hours after that came work. "Listen, I'd love to stay and chat, but I have to be up early this morning."

Karen checked her watch too. "Yeah. Me too. How about dinner tonight?"

I was slamdunked. Rarely had I been on the receiving end of a date request. Almost inevitably, I did the asking and performed the standard, regretful shake of the head when I was turned down. So, I mumbled, "Sure." Took down the time—7 P.M.—and the place—some downtown bistro named Bangkok Palace II—and stumbled out before waking up from the dream.

Watching her leave the thinning crowd, I wondered what fate had brought me to her. Something resembling hope started to creep up in my chest, but the cynic in me stomped it back down again. Despite Stephen King's assurances to the contrary, hope never got anybody anywhere. My brother's Puritan expression floated in the air, and I listened as he counseled me, "You never took my advice about women, Duffy. That's always been your problem. Women are evil. You just have to find one that's less evil than the others."

Thanks, bro, I thought as the apparition faded into a case of lemon-flavored Perrier stacked in the aisle. But, once again, I fully intended to ignore his advice.

Back at the ranch, it appeared from close observation that Kirby's river of guests had dried up. Should be able to corral the little fellow, I thought, just lock him in his room and get some shut-eye. So, I slipped in the front door to a dark living room, another sign that the night's activities were finally over, and I began to be hopeful that roping Kirby wouldn't be necessary. But, after I closed the door behind me, I saw a faint glow from around the corner, and I smelled a vaguely familiar sweet odor hanging in the air, something other than the dirty socks I'd left by the couch.

A single female, wearing an outfit that looked like something out of a 1960s sitcom, sat in the lotus position meditating in front of a tall, red candle. A hand-rolled cigarette dangled from her puffy lips. Stringy brunette hair brushed its tips against her shoulders, and in the glow of the light, I saw lines running deeply at the corners of her eyes. Definitely from the "been around the block more than once" school of womanhood.

Wanting to ask a number of questions—like what was a woman like this doing smoking hashish in my living room—I remembered that my bedroom door had a lock on it. Since discretion has always seemed like the best road to honor, valor, and all those other virtues, I opted to ignore her and slide quietly into my room. I'd finally get some sleep, and hopefully it would be Karen haunting my dreams, not Abdulmohsen, orange-coveralled Bangladeshis, or dope-smoking women.

"Who the fuck are you?"

The voice! That voice! I knew it! Slightly cracked, hoarse from pouring Jack Daniels down her throat for the last couple of decades, words slurred and drawn out in that inimitable southern Kentucky/middle Tennessee twang.

I stopped and looked at her. Nope. Never seen her before in my life, and, yet, I'd seen thousands of her all my life. It was the type, not the girl, that was familiar.

"I said, who the fuck are you?" She said "fuck" like it had three syllables.

"Duffy. Who are you?"

She took a hit off the joint, sucked in deep, and expelled a little smoke before answering. "Ah'm Debbie. Where ya'll from?"

"Nashville. You?"

She nodded. "Bowling Green. You know Kirby, too?" Debbie closed her eyes and began swaying to some kind of internal, twenty-four-hour music station.

"In a way. I'm his roommate." I edged toward the hallway and my room, still planning to lock myself away.

But Debbie, sweet 7-11 Debbie, must have had the most sensitive hearing in the world, because she opened her eyes in surprise at the nearly silent shuffle of my feet on the carpet. "Hey, nowww. Don't leave me."

"Got to. Early day today."

She stopped swaying and smiled. "Hey, you wanna fuck?"

"That what you do for Kirby?"

"That's what I do for money, silly. But, you?" She looked me up and down, and a knot grew in my stomach as the smile broadened. "I'll give you a freebie cause you're from back home. Kirby? Not lessen he pays, but he ain't never paid. I ain't sure he has sex—just sits there and asks me stupid questions. But, hey," she said, taking another toke on the joint, "he's got great shit to smoke. Beats the hell out of that Kentucky stuff. So, long as he's got the hash, I'll let him ask questions. Even if it is my night off. So, you want to do it?"

I hadn't seen the inside of my eyelids for too long. "Next time, baby. Right now, Daddy's got to ride the Valium train. Maybe sometime I'll come over and we'll do all the things I never got to do with the hogs back home."

She smiled again, and I noticed a broken tooth. "You're on, sugar."

What in the hell was Kirby up to?

CHAPTER
SIX

The next morning, I tried to talk to Kirby over coffee and bagels. In a fit of decency the night before, I'd picked up a can of one of those designer coffees and some Kuwaiti-baked bagels—which I thought was a little strange since bagels are identified most closely with Jews. But, who was I to deny anybody a little ethnic food? Anyway, I got up about a half hour before Kirby, and I made a little coffee, nuked some bagels, split 'em and tossed 'em on a couple of little plates.

After first reconning the situation, I determined that Debbie was not still in the vicinity (although the red candle still stood erect on the coffee table), and proceeded with my plan, which included sweeping the red candle onto the floor. For just a few minutes, I thought about buying a phone card—Kuwaiti international phone lines run about $1,500 each, so the prepaid phone card was the only logical option—and reporting her to the Search for Extra-Terrestrial Intelligence program, but I didn't want to waste the money.

I laid all the stuff out and waited for the sound of a flushing toilet. After several minutes of ominous belching and grumbling from Kirby's end of the suite, I heard the all-too-familiar lyrics of water racing down the toilet bowl and a door rattle open.

A smile crouched on my face as Kirby appeared in the hallway. God! What a miserable sight. Hair poked and protruded from the top of his head, from his ears, from his mustache. His morning beard reminded me of coarse sandpaper. As a distinctly unpleasant odor slipped down the hallway, I pulled my cup of hazelnut coffee closer to my nose, trying to mask the Kirby smell.

"What the hell is this? Did you use my dishes?" Kirby looked crazed.

"Jesus, Kirby. I just fixed us a little breakfast. Have you always been wound up this tight?"

He grumbled a second, shifting from one foot to the other. I noticed that he had Mickey Mouse boxers on. "Sorry, sorry," he said with something resembling apology in his tone. "Bagels, huh? Yeah, I like bagels." Kirby plopped down on the couch and sniffed the coffee. "What is this?"

"Hazelnut. I thought it would be a decent change from Folger's."

Kirby's beady little eyes narrowed even further, which was quite a feat. "Why are you doing this? You're not like Perry Howell, are you? This isn't some kind of come-on, is it?"

"No, Kirby. I'm not like Perry Howell. This is not a come-on. Believe me, even if I was gay, you wouldn't be my type."

His eyes shot up over the cup, piercing me with the intensity. "Why not?"

"That has nothing to do with the topic at hand."

He thought about that one for a second. "What's the topic at hand?" Obviously, I had him stumped.

"Who is this Debbie chick?"

The very thought of Kirby Benson's eyebrows wrinkling together is one of mammoth proportions, but that's what they did, making his forehead look like the Rocky Mountains with hair. "Who's Debbie?"

"C'mon, Kirby. The girl here in the living room last night. The one you fixed up with hashish."

Then came the parting of the eyebrows that ranked right up there with the parting of the Red Sea. A wide gap opened up and the wrinkles smoothed immediately. "Oh, the whore. So, what about her?"

"You don't even know her name, and she's smoking shit in our living room?"

He waved me off, jamming a bagel in his mouth. "Yeah, yeah," he mumbled. "I knew it was Betty or Debbie or something like that. She's part of my research."

"What are you working on?" It came out before I realized it. The last thing I wanted was an intimate knowledge of anything Kirby Benson was working on.

Fortunately, my insistent tone just put Kirby on guard. "ABSOLUTELY NOT! It's none of your business." He tossed the bagel on the coffee table and jumped up, his jowls jiggling in response. "You want to steal my idea. You want to steal my story!"

———

Work that day turned out to be just as unpleasant. I asked Fitzy on the way in if Frank was going to make it to the office.

"Are you kidding? Frank won't be back until he finishes off all the junk that Perry brought back. That'll take a good week anyway."

"So what are we gonna do about this thing at the base?"

"What thing?"

"You know, the problem Major Nasser brought up."

"Oh, yeah, that. Don't worry. It'll go away."

"How's that?"

"Awwh," Fitzy said, shaking his head. "The Kuwaitis are always complaining about something. Then they forget about it for a couple of months."

Fitzy wore a frown, like he was pissed that I'd brought the subject up, so I let it die a quiet death. Always time later to address it again, I thought. Of course, that was before PFC Jufain Al-Subaie pulled an M-16 on Perry Howell.

I was playing Minesweeper on the computer and Fitzy was doing the crossword in the *Arab Times* when the screaming started. For once in my life, I reacted without stopping to think about it. Knocking over two chairs and stepping on George in the process, I still managed to beat Fitzy down the hall.

The screaming grew louder, and several classroom doors popped open, instructors sticking their heads out as I flew past.

From the crowd gathered outside Room 4, I figured that must be the scene of the disaster. Out the door, I could see three or four Kuwaiti officers racing out of battalion headquarters toward our building.

I pushed a couple of guys out of the way as the screaming approached deafening proportions. Struggling between two pretty beefy boys, I found myself in the doorway and came as close as I ever have to complete and total panic.

PFC Jufain Al-Subaie, a stocky kid with a perpetually stupid grin on his face, held an M-16, magazine inserted, on Perry Howell, who cowered unsuccessfully behind a chair at the front of the room. Most of the screaming came from Perry, but Jufain was adding his own deep bass to the squawling. Something like, "*Inta Haram! Inta Haram!*"

"What's he saying?" I asked a kid next to me. The boy just smiled, and I realized he didn't understand the question.

"He's telling Mr. Perry that he is *haram*, forbidden," said a soft voice at my elbow. I glanced back to see Major Nasser.

We wedged our way into the room, and I saw that Jufain's finger was indeed on the trigger. I also saw a little puddle of a strange yellow liquid edging out from under the chair.

"Jufain!" I elbowed Nasser in the side. "Translate for me."

"Why?" he pointed out. "He recognizes his name."

"Good point. Jufain, what's wrong? Why are you doing this?"

Nasser obediently rattled off the Arabic version.

Jufain began shouting, pushing the muzzle at Perry with each exclamation.

"*Tayyeb*; okay," Nasser said, turning to me. "He says that Mr. Perry offered to give him a blowjob at lunch. Jufain is a very good Muslim, and he was offended. This is his way of seeking the return of his honor."

"Jufain, Jufain, Jufain," I repeated the guy's name so many times because, frankly, I didn't know what else to say. "Listen, Jufain, look under the desk. He's already pissed on himself. Isn't that satisfaction enough?" Then, a sudden chauvinistic impulse struck me. "And see how he did it? Squatting like a woman."

Nasser spoke quickly, in what seemed to be appropriate Arabic; a smile spread across Jufain's face, and the muzzle dropped an inch. Two other officers appeared in the door, but Nasser held up a hand.

"Killing him serves no purpose. His cowardice steals his honor and restores yours."

Again, my interpreter made the required sounds. Jufain dropped the muzzle completely now, handed me the weapon and walked out of the room with a chuckle. Two other officers raced after him, but I made a quick M-16 handoff to one of the other students and double-timed to catch up.

"Hey, guys! Give the kid a break. I'd have probably done the same thing."

"He's right," interrupted Major Nasser. "Let Jufain go. Punishing him will serve no purpose."

The crowd dispersed, and I saw Perry sneaking off to the toilet. Nasser grabbed my arm. "Walk with me, Duffy. Where are you from?"

"Tennessee, sir."

"Were you an English teacher in the United States?"

"At one time. I've also done a little bit of everything else too."

A group of airmen scattered before us as we stopped beneath a eucalyptus tree. Nasser lit a cigarette and leaned against the tree. "Tell me, Duffy. What do you think of this operation?"

That was a question I wasn't prepared to answer. "Well, Major, I've been at work a total of a day and a half. A little early to be making judgments."

Nasser nodded. "Anyone else would have assured me how wonderful everything is. Let me tell you something, Duffy. It is my job to make sure that these boys speak English well enough to go to the states. There they will learn how to operate the Patriot missile batteries. And that will make my country better prepared if anyone crosses her borders again. I will do anything necessary to make sure that everything happens as it should. But, understand that I know the difficulty of the task. I know also that you have talented teachers among you. But even talented teachers need leadership and guidance.

"I served in the Gulf War, and I saw a multitude of leaders, some good, some bad. Watching you back there, I saw a man who wears leadership easily, like an old coat. Men instinctively look to you. They are comfortable under your guidance."

"Is this going somewhere, Major?" I smelled trouble.

He smiled. "See. You do not hesitate to cut through the bullshit. Yes, this is going somewhere. If we have to cancel this contract, it will set us back two years. That will leave my country—my family—more vulnerable. That is unacceptable to me. Until you showed up yesterday, I had almost resigned myself to the unacceptable. Now, I see a chance to get this thing back on course."

"Wait a minute, Major. You can't hang this problem around my neck. What about Fitzy?"

"Fitzy," Nasser shrugged, "is a good boy. But he is too hot-tempered, too impulsive, and too much Frank's boy. I've watched the dynamics. You are new, too new to be on anybody's side. The others will trust you where they'll never trust Frank and Fitzy."

"You still haven't given me one good reason not to hop the first flight out of here."

"I'll give you two reasons. First, if you give up on this program, you give up not just on yourself, but on your colleagues, and on Kuwait. I don't think you can live with that. Not when you can make a difference." He paused.

"Yeah? And the second reason?"

He flipped his cigarette to the ground and mashed it into the sand with his shoe. "You must have the permission of the Kuwaiti government to leave the country. It's called an exit letter. You may find it difficult to get one, at least any time soon." Major Nasser looked up and patted me on the shoulder. "Don't worry, Duffy. You may grow to like it here." Shoving his hands in his pockets, he wandered off toward headquarters, his shoulders held straight, firm, like an athlete confident in his performance.

I chose to kick the eucalyptus tree.

CHAPTER
SEVEN

Bangkok Garden II was a narrow walk-up behind the Al-Muthana Complex, a combination shopping mall and apartment building, in the middle of downtown Kuwait City. The buildings nearby housed matchbook-sized Indian and Pakistani restaurants, and the cloying odor of curry hung in the air. Thai food was dwarfed in popularity.

"You're certainly a pleasure to be around tonight," Karen said.

"It just wasn't a good day," I said finally. All my excitement, all my enthusiasm at seeing Karen again had been blasted out of the sky as efficiently as a Patriot missile took out a Scud. Major Nasser knew his job well.

"Want to talk about it?" The question was sincere.

"I'm not sure what to say." How do you explain that you talked a Muslim, seeking the return of his honor from an American homosexual, out of his rifle? And, as a result, you were informed by a Kuwaiti officer that you would be held in

Kuwait until hell or Kuwait froze over. Even in his brightest moment, I'm not sure that Einstein could have made his theory of relativity work in Kuwait.

So, I told her. Frank. Perry. Kirby. Debbie. Alcohol and drug addiction. Pedophilia. Paranoid-schizophrenics. Opium-smoking prostitutes. The terror in Perry's eyes as he contemplated the muzzle of Jufain's M-16. Major Nasser's less-than-veiled threats. I even told her about stepping on George as I rushed to disarm Jufain. It was . . . it was . . . absolutely and completely cathartic.

Although Karen's expression didn't waver over the course of my confession, her slightly full lips did purse a bit at the end. "How long have you been in Kuwait?" she asked.

I looked at my watch. "Oh, about five days."

She jumped in with a little laugh, reaching after a second across the table and cupping my hands in hers. They were soft and delicate, the fingers curving ever so slightly around mine. She wore a gold band with a heart-shaped design on her right ring finger. "Poor Duffy. Did anything in life prepare you for what you've seen in five days here?"

She slipped a compact from her purse and touched up her nose quickly and efficiently. "This country defies description. Look," she commanded, putting away the compact. "Here's an example. We had an NGO, nongovernmental organization, a nonprofit educational outfit that holds the United States Information Service contract for advising. They needed to move to a new building for a variety of reasons. Now, the head honcho of our NGO went down to the Kuwait Municipality Board to get approval for a villa over in Jabriyah. In one office, the Kuwaiti official checked out the request letter, glanced in a file on his desk, and handed the request back with a smile. 'No problem,' he said. 'You're not a commercial operation. You can move wherever you want.'

"So, the honcho decided that he should check one more office there, just to be on the safe side. Down the hall, in an identical office, sat an almost identical Kuwaiti official. He read the letter, glanced in a file, and handed it back with a frown. 'Permission denied. That area is not open to commercial businesses,' he said.

"'Wait a minute,' the honcho said. 'The guy down the hall in Room 210 said that we could move.' The Kuwaiti shrugged and said, 'So?' 'Well,' our hero asked, 'is he right or wrong?' 'He's right,' answered the Kuwaiti. 'So,' the NGO guy said, 'if we ask him and he says it's okay, it's okay. But, if we ask you and you say no, then we can't.' 'Right,' smiled the Kuwaiti. The NGO guy grabbed the letter and said, 'Sorry to have bothered you. I never came in here. Goodbye.' And that was that. They moved.

"Kuwait is like Neverland," Karen continued. "I fully expect to look out the window and see Peter and Tinkerbelle floating along."

"Well, at least the Tinkerbelle part is right. At least three-quarters of our staff have to be flamers."

A concerned look tightened her lips. "That doesn't include you, I trust?"

I shook my head more than vigorously. "Absolutely not. I like my sex the way I like my vodka. Straight up."

"That's a relief. I thought I'd lost my touch." I noticed that my heart took off at a dead run.

"What do you think Kirby is up to?" After a second's pause, she redirected the conversation.

I shrugged. "With Kirby he could be within hours of breaking a story on Kuwait's nuclear weapon capability, or . . ."

"Or what?"

"Or, a hot news flash that the Allies won the Second World War. I'm not sure Kirby can tell the difference. He sort of fades in and out of reality."

"It would be interesting to know if he's really onto something."
My eyes narrowed appropriately. "Am I hearing Karen, the
diplomat?"

"I guess. But, you've got to admit that the whole thing
sounds fascinating. Kuwaitis, Bangladeshis, American prostitutes. Kirby's threats that it will bring down two administrations. If you find out anything more, let me know. The ambassador might like a bedtime story."

"Does that indicate that you tuck him in every night?" Before she could answer, a waitress floated by with a Virginia Slim
barely holding its grip on her lips; I grabbed her. "Did you
send to Bangkok, Chiang Mai, or Phuket for our dinners?"

"Soon. Soon," she answered, dropping a cylinder of ashes
on my shoulder.

"You are a real charmer. First, you accuse me of sleeping
with the ambassador—a charge, I might add, that his wife
would not appreciate. Then, you accost an innocent waitress
and demand your order. Is this the famous Tennessee hospi-
tality I've heard so much about?"

"No," I replied honestly. "This is the famous jaded attitude
so common among men of my age."

"Speaking from personal experience?" Only a half-tease
hung in the question, so I picked my answer carefully.

"Only from having watched a number of my male friends
attempt to juggle two and sometimes three women at the same
time."

She drew her head back in almost mock surprise. "Three?
Is that ambition or hyperactivity?"

"Probably both." I twisted around, looking to see if a Pony
Express rider was delivering our dinner.

"Would you quit worrying about food? Look, I know it's
been a rough day." She stopped. "Why don't we dump this

joint, go back to my place, and let me doctor you with a little vodka. If you get really hungry, we can always order Chinese. How did you get here?"

"Bus."

She took my hand. "C'mon. I'll drive."

———◆———

Karen lived in a beautiful townhouse near the old U.S. Embassy in Bneid Al Gar. The row of houses resembled a line of dominoes, each set slightly forward and overlapping the one behind it. As we drove across the bumpy sand field in front of her place, she pointed at a brown brick building, sitting behind a battered wall. It was eerily dark, all the windows broken, and a flagpole, shattered in half, lay teetering over the front façade. "The Iraqi Embassy," she explained. "They trashed it pretty bad during the liberation."

I just nodded. In the few days I'd been there, I'd begun to get used to the armored cars parked at traffic lights, .50-caliber machine guns mounted on top. A few buildings still showed battle damage, but there were signs of repair everywhere you turned, except here, at the Iraqi Embassy. In some ways, I guess you could say it was the last Iraqi casualty of the war. Not that I could blame the Kuwaitis. Fitzy had a buddy who was a policeman, and we stopped at the police station in Salmiya one day to hunt him down. They had photographs on the walls of burned corpses in the middle of the street. A police lieutenant wandered up next to me as I looked at them. "That was my cousin," he said. "The Iraqis dragged him out of his car, poured gasoline on him, and set him on fire. He was sixteen." After that, I had a tough time mustering any sympathy for the forlorn Iraqi Embassy.

Karen held the gate open for me, locking it back carefully behind us. An Indian man stood in the doorway. "Hello, Miss Karen."

"John, this is Mr. Duffy. He needs a vodka tonic right away or he may die."

John's face became suddenly serious. "Yes, ma'am." And he spun on his heel, disappearing inside the house. We trudged up the steps behind him.

"John is incredibly loyal," Karen pointed out. "So don't even think about questioning him about the number and kind of gentlemen I've entertained."

The townhouse was magnificent, compared to my quarters, which only last week seemed adequate—if you subtracted Kirby, that is. A square-built staircase was to the immediate right. Beyond that was the living room. From the second floor, you could look right down on the living area. Sort of reminded me of the balcony in a theater-in-the-round. Picasso prints decorated the walls above the sofas and side chairs. A coffee table and end tables, deep burnished walnut, fronted and flanked the chairs.

"Let's not stint on our diplomats' comfort," I said, a little louder than I intended, and even from the furthest corner of my eye, I saw Karen stiffen.

"Sorry, sorry. It's that taxpayer in me. You know, the ingrained, habitual complaints of the American taxpayer." I rushed the words out even as I was turning to face her.

Her frown cracked into another smile before I'd finished. "Hey, brains. I hate to break this to you, but you're not a taxpayer anymore." She looked around, the brown hair flying around her shoulders. "In fact," she continued. "I seem to be the only taxpayer in the room."

John appeared out of the kitchen with our drinks before I could come up with a brilliant reply.

The vodka tonic tasted good going down, cold and clean, well, clean in comparison to ethanol. I took a long gulp and then sank onto a couch. Karen followed suit, her long slender fingers holding the drink lightly, even tenderly.

"So what happened to your marriage, Duffy?"

"Fell apart on me."

"And who gets the blame for that?"

I hit the vodka tonic and considered the question. "Placing blame isn't in my portfolio. It happened." The sofa shifted under me, and I knew she had moved, but I didn't look to see which way.

"Sounds like a slick way to duck the blame."

Boy, this girl didn't waste time or breath. "Do you always go for the jugular?"

"It's my gift. I also think that moping around and feeling guilty about a screwed-up relationship is the quickest way to doom any future relationships. Nothing is ever absolute, Duffy. Nothing is ever 100 percent. Accept the percentage of the blame that falls on you, try to learn from it, and move on."

The vodka began washing away my nerves, taking the shiver from my hand. "Okay. I'm 99 percent to blame." The sofa shifted again under me, and this time I looked to see her just inches away. She reached over and pulled the glass from my hand, putting it on the coffee table.

"I don't think it's quite that easy, Duffy. But we can work on it."

~⌣~

The next morning, I whistled to myself in the gentle breeze as I headed to Fitzy's Swiftie. Before the sun climbed too high in the sky, Kuwait could be pleasant, especially if the wind blew in from the east, carrying with it the light, pleasant taste of the salt of the Arabian Gulf. It felt so good that I stopped beside the car and leaned back, just to take it all in.

"Where were you last night?" The scratchy voice couldn't be mistaken: Kirby Benson, in all his cigarette-hoarsened glory. He stumbled across the parking lot, a frown stretching his pitted face and mustache into a cross between Groucho Marx and a gargoyle.

The good feeling coursing through my veins reversed direction. "How about, 'good morning, Duffy'? Do you have to jump into the inquisition without the proper social amenities?"

That stopped Kirby dead. "What's an amenity?"

"Never mind. I had some things to do last night, okay?" Fitzy bounced out of the building and strutted across the lot toward us.

"No! No! No! I will not leave it. Debbie, or Donna, or whatever her name is was over last night and wanted to see you. It didn't matter what I offered her; she wouldn't talk unless I could produce you."

"Sounds like you have a personal problem, Kirby. Maybe you should take it to the chaplain." I was trying hard to ignore him.

"You will not interfere with my research. I'll not have it. You have to stay home tonight and talk to Diana." Kirby's jowls jiggled with irritation.

Before I could really let Kirby have it, Fitzy made it to the car. "Benson, fuck off! Time to go to work."

Kirby shuffled off to one of the other cars.

I climbed in with Fitzy and he gave me a dirty look. "Where *were* you last night?"

"What the hell is this? Is there some kind of curfew nobody told me about?"

Fitzy shook his head. "No. But Serge was looking for you. He's having a big party tonight. Bunch of bozos from the Russian parliament are in town. Anyway, he wants us to be there." Fitzy beamed from ear to ear, visions of vodka bottles dancing across his brain.

That was interesting. A diplomatic soirée. Maybe Karen would go with me. "What time?"

"Ten."

"A little late for a party, no?"

"Not in Kuwait. Perry's not coming in today, so it'll be just you and me."

"What's wrong with Perry?"

Fitzy shrugged. He made it into an art form, starting the shrug with his shoulders slowly and then letting it build in intensity until, at the very height, his head joined in, cocking itself to one side. "Who knows? Maybe he got a dick stuck in his ass."

"What about Frank? Still down with, uh, strep throat?"

"Yeah," Fitzy said with a laugh. "Drank a quart of ethanol last night. He'll be lucky to see sunlight today. Oh, by the way, you're getting Fuzzball's car tonight."

"What's a Fuzzball, and why did he have a car?"

Fitzy frowned for half a second before minor recognition struck his eyes. "Oh, yeah, that's right. You're new. Fuzzball was this guy they sent over for a couple of weeks. He was supposed to be a senior instructor, but one night he slammed his car into a light pole at the airport and the last anybody saw of him he was rushing through passport control. Anyway, we just got his car back from the shop."

Sounded like I could learn a few things from Fuzzball.

I considered telling Fitzy about my conversation with Major Nasser, but just as the words started to come out, I dammed them up. Nothing to be gained, I realized, by saying anything. It certainly wouldn't get my prison sentence reduced. Maybe, I mused, Jufain would bring his M-16 and shoot me. That thought, at least, put the smile back on my face. Life is funny, you know. The highs are so high and the lows are so low. I just wish there was a middle ground.

—◡—

"So, anything happen at work today? Nobody got shot or molested, I hope." Karen's voice was filled with sarcasm.

"No. I did virtually nothing but play solitaire. Well, that's only partially true. Perry Howell tracked me down after work and offered to give me a blowjob for getting Jufain's M-16 out of his face."

"Did you accept?"

"Of course I didn't. I simply explained to him that if he even suggested such an activity again, I'd flush him down the enlisted men's toilet. You coming to the party with me or not?"

A pause marked the other end of the phone. "Russian Duma members?"

"Yeah. And, hey, I even have my own set of wheels now."

"That's comforting." She paused and I heard her take a breath or two on the other end. "I guess it'll be okay. But I'll have to tell my section head. Just to be on the safe side, you understand."

"And which section do you work for? The CIA?"

"No. They rejected me."

"We all have our bad days," I consoled. "So, be over about 9:30, okay?" I gave her directions and said goodbye, and a little shiver of warning ran through my aging bones.

This thing with Karen was moving a little too fast for my liking. Well, hell, that wasn't it either. It was exactly to my liking, and it was completely uncomfortable, primarily because it was incredibly comfortable. I sat on the edge of my bed and stared at the telephone, tempted to call her back and make some excuse, canceling the evening. But the thought of Serge and his antics and the taste of good Russian Stolichnaya were enough to tug my hand away from the receiver.

Falling backward on the bed, I thought about crying. All my life, it seemed like, I'd been put in situations that everybody else thought I was amply qualified for, and that, if the truth be told, I was sadly unqualified for. Kuwait was proving to be no different from anywhere else.

I didn't come to Kuwait to be anybody's savior. I mean, I had enough trouble saving myself. That much I figured I could handle, at least marginally. But, I sure as hell didn't come to Kuwait to save the Patriot missile project, or the whole damned country. Major Nasser needed some lessons in human resource development; my résumé hardly qualified me as Joan of Arc.

〜

"Why do I feel like Daniella walking into the lion's den?" Karen said, straightening her dress as I knocked on Serge's door.

"Duffy! Welcome!" I was engulfed by Serge's massive arms. For just a second, I thought I was going to be suffocated in the hair on his chest, but fortunately the thick gold chain around his neck gave me a little breathing room. "And who is this?" he said, releasing me and looking Karen up and down with a wink.

"Karen, meet Serge. Serge, meet Karen."

Karen extended her hand. "We've met before. Karen Solomon, from the U.S. consular staff."

Serge smiled even more broadly. "Of course. You came to our National Day. Duffy, you have excellent taste in women. *Walla*! I swear it! Come into my flat. Please!"

Fitzy was already there, a shot of vodka in hand. Must have been fifteen people scattered through the dining area and living room, every one of them with drink in hand. Well, except for this one man, a big, heavyset, Joe Stalin look-alike. He had a drink in each hand, knocking them back like they were lemonade. Linna, Serge's wife, stood over him with a bottle of Stoli, filling his glass every time it emptied.

"Serge?" I elbowed the Russian in the side. "Who's the drunk with the big mustache?"

A belly-deep laugh rumbled around Serge's throat. "That is Igor Vasilikov, leader of the nationalist movement. He likes vodka almost as much as he hates Americans."

"So, why did you invite us if he hates Americans?"

"Because the ambassador hates Igor more than he hates Americans. 'Sergei,' he told me, 'make Igor Mikhailovich as angry as you can. Maybe he will not come back here.' So, I invited you and Fitzy. *Walla*, I swear it."

The idea of being a tool of Russian internal politics was less than appealing, but I held my tongue.

Serge patted me on the back. "Have some—how do you say it—appetizers. *Da*. That's it. Appetizers."

Steering Karen toward the table, my stomach clenched at the sight of all these little red and green things wrapped in tiny fish filets, the silver skin still intact. "What are those?"

"You'll never make a diplomat," Karen hissed.

"Let me get this straight. The essence of diplomacy is to eat food that looks like it should still be swimming in the Gulf?"

"The essence of diplomacy," she responded, "is something I'm afraid will forever elude you."

I snatched up one of the fish roll things and popped it in my mouth. The burn started fast and spread around my mouth and down my throat. "Jesus!" I coughed. "What the hell is this?"

"I have no idea," Karen confessed, sniffing at one she held gingerly between two fingers. "Here, don't let me be a glutton. You eat it." And she shoved it in my mouth just as I opened it to protest.

Another wave of jalapeño-caliber heat stormed down my throat, and I choked again. Through tear-blurred eyes, I could see Karen looking quite pleased with herself. Then, a hammer came slamming down on my back.

I spun around to see the barrel-chested Igor pounding his giant fist into the trough between my shoulder blades.

"Are—you—okay?" he stuttered in slow English.

"Yeah, I think so," I managed to get out. "Thanks."

"You are American?"

"That's what my birth certificate says."

"*Da. Da.* Good, very good. I will speak to you." Igor laughed, although it sounded more like a belch. "This is your woman?" He pointed to Karen, who frowned in return.

"This is my friend."

"Same—same."

"Not quite. Karen Solomon." She pushed her hand forward, forcing a smile. "U.S. Embassy."

Igor's smile faded to a frown. "Diplomats." The way he said it was, well, priceless. And as if he sensed my own basic, gut-level reaction, Igor turned to me and sadly shook his mammoth head. "They will ruin the world. But, since she is with you, I will speak to her too."

"How kind of you," Karen replied through clenched teeth, then in an aside to me, "Isn't there a leash law in Kuwait?"

Igor nodded compassionately. "Diplomats talk too much and do nothing. But you, you are a typical American working man, *da*?"

Well, that stopped me in my tracks. I'd changed careers about four times. Married and divorced. Owed everything I made as well as most of any offspring I might have to credit card companies. "Yeah, I guess you're right," I finally agreed.

"*Da! Da!* An American who speaks the truth! What is your job, Mr. American?" Igor belched at the end, almost in harmony with the question, and the liver- and lung-curdling scent of bad cigars and vodka-marinated appetizers engulfed me.

"He is an English teacher," Serge said, sweeping in between us and wrapping an arm around my shoulder. Igor frowned at Serge's sudden appearance. "Igor Mikhailovich, there is more wodka to drink. Do not be . . . How do you say it?" he asked me.

"Bashful?"

"*Da!* Bashful!"

Igor grumbled, but struggled off toward a bottle somebody had made the mistake of setting down. "English teacher," he muttered as he walked off.

"See you around the Kremlin, Igor. Leave some vodka for later," I said, but Serge pulled me away.

"It does no good to argue with him," Serge said. "The more wodka he drinks the more he argues." He turned to Karen. "You are having good time?"

She looked at the recently departed Igor with bottle turned up, vodka draining down his throat like rain through a gutter, and at another Russian, this one's hand firmly planted on the bottom of Serge's daughter. "You can really throw a party, Sergei," she finally answered. I sensed something undiplomatic about to part her lips, so I deftly turned her around and shoved her in Fitzy's direction. The later it got, the dimmer the lights became, and, I noticed without a lot of surprise, couples started disappearing into the bedrooms.

"Duffy," Karen began. "This party is getting a little out of hand." She pointed toward the living room where one of the other females had proceeded to take off her blouse, swinging it happily around her head. "How am I going to explain it to the ambassador if I get arrested at a Russian's orgy? I like you a lot, Duffy, but I'm not going to lose my job just to babysit you."

"I'll come with you."

Karen shook her head firmly. "Not tonight, pal. I'll call you." I stared at the door a good ninety seconds, until I felt a heavy arm drape over my shoulder.

"Duffy! This is no way to party. Forget the woman. I find you another one. Besides, we have wodka to drink. Come, come!" And I followed Serge back to the table where another bottle of Stolichnaya had appeared.

Fitzy ceremoniously slammed a shot glass of ice-cold vodka on the table in front of me. "This," he said with great feeling, "is the cure for all ills." Serge nodded enthusiastically as I watched Igor collapse on the other side of the room.

CHAPTER
EIGHT

I was down by then, really down, so I followed Serge's example. Igor spent a lot of time smacking me on the back as I got the hang of shooting ice-cold vodka. Fitzy joined in, and thirty minutes later, we were drunk. And some time after midnight, I nodded off.

Later, I remember hearing a soft, pitiful whimper. Not like a beaten puppy, but not completely unlike that either. I opened my eyes and glanced around—Fitzy had collapsed on the table and was sleeping among the varieties of herring. Igor was still lying on the floor in front of the television, a vodka bottle cradled lovingly in his arms. A couple of other Duma guys were out under the dining table. I was propped up against the end of a couch. The whimpering continued, and I tried to focus on the sound.

It was Serge, sitting on a couch across the living room, head in hands, rocking like an autistic child. Linna was not in evidence.

"Serge, man, are you okay?" I rolled to one side in a feeble attempt to get up.

His big blond head shook, and a shaft of light flooding in from the kitchen sparkled off tears on his cheek. "You cannot know, Duffy." His breath came in staggered bursts.

At that particular moment, I didn't want to know anything but a pillow against my head. I checked my watch—4 A.M. My second week in Kuwait, the land of temperance, and I'd succeeded in staying drunk all night for the second time. But I have this annoying streak of compassion running through me, so I had to ask, "What's wrong, Serge?"

He straightened his shoulders and frowned. "Marina, my daughter."

"Oh, yeah, you want her to learn English." I wasn't really listening; I was more interested in getting into an upright position.

"No. No. She never tells me where she's going."

"Teenagers are like that." On my knees now, I could see victory in my grasp.

"This is different, Duffy. *Walla*, I swear it. I'm very worried about her. Marina goes out and stays out all night."

"She'll grow out of it." One foot was firmly planted, and I just needed a Saturn rocket to get the other one placed.

"I need your help, Duffy."

"You're the Russian consul, Serge. Get your people to follow her."

"I can't."

I was working up the energy for blastoff. "Why not?"

"I am, how do you say, short-listed, *da*, short-listed for ambassador. I cannot go to the security people. It would be a big problem for me. If Marina is involved in bad things, my career it would be *zifft*." This word I recognized. *Zifft* in Arabic means "nothing," "less than nothing."

"And she is my daughter, Duffy. I am afraid. You were a policeman."

"I—am—an—English—teacher, Serge." I said the words slowly and distinctly, hoping they penetrated the vodka curtain closing off his brain. "What the hell can I do?"

He frowned. "You can find out what she does. I have no one else to turn to."

"What about Fitzy?"

"Fitzy is my friend, but he is young. And he listens to music too loud. I need someone who has—how you say it—been around the block. I need you."

Getting drunk with a Russian diplomat was one thing; being recruited to shadow his daughter on her midnight excursions was a camel of a completely different color. And besides, I'd almost made it up with both feet. Escape seemed imminent.

"Serge, man, you don't even know me. I could be CIA."

"No, you couldn't be," Serge said with a sad smile.

"Why not?"

"You show signs of intelligence."

"If that's your logic, it's no wonder you lost the Cold War. Surely your own people keep you under surveillance."

"I have kept them out of my personal problems."

"How?" The very idea of keeping the KGB or whatever they called it these days out of a consul's business was, at best, humorous.

"That is not for you to concern yourself. Please, Duffy, I beg you. I am worried about my daughter."

I've always been a sucker for crying parents. I never had a kid; the closest my wife ever came was a miscarriage at six months. We named her though, named her and buried her in the family plot. I never went up there again. And now, six thousand miles away, I couldn't help but think about her again, the daughter that might have been. Other thoughts blew through too, like maybe Serge was trying to compromise me. But then I looked at him again, and all I saw was a father who really cared about his kid, and what good could it do to compromise me? What did I know? I wasn't even sure that getting in out of the rain was in my repertoire.

"Okay, Serge," I said finally. "All right. I'll see what I can do." Usually, I'd been told, it was the fathers you had to worry about out here in the land of Islam. They kept close tabs on their daughters to keep infidel scumbags like me away from them. Well, this time I had the father's permission. So, what harm could come of it? Obviously, I wasn't playing with a full deck.

Work the next day, or rather, later that same day, became an exercise in futility. After four cups of coffee and ten Panadol, I arrived at a small semblance of alertness. Kirby spent every spare moment ragging me about abandoning him again. The dialogue went something like this:

"You don't care about me anymore," Kirby whined.

"I never cared about you, Kirby. Leave me alone."

"You were out with Fitzy getting drunk."

"Yes. And now I have the hangover from hell. Leave me to my misery."

"But," and the whining reached beyond annoying into obnoxious. "I need you, so Deirdre—"

"—Debbie—"

"—whatever, will tell me what she knows."

A pounding headache, dry, vodka-tainted mouth, and blurred vision outranked all of Kirby's priorities. "Go away, Kirby. Let me die in peace."

Fitzy appeared over my shoulder about that time doing a passable imitation of a Catholic priest administering the last rites—Requiescat In Pace, or whatever. "You sure you're not half-Russian?" he asked on one pass.

"My blood right now is about 50 percent Stolichnaya, so maybe that's accounting for your confusion. Leave me alone, Fitzy," I commanded, dropping my head to the desk.

"No," Fitzy droned on above me. "The reason I say that is because I've never, ever seen an American that can shoot vodka with a Russian and match him shot for shot."

"Great men," I explained patiently, "are just ordinary men faced with extraordinary challenges. Now leave me alone."

After work, I hit the elevator with a passion, banging the button as hard as I could. My bed called, and the elevator was in a conspiracy to deprive me of sleep. After an interminable minute, the door flew open, revealing Marina in the arms of a teenage Arab getting a tonsillectomy. Lothario seemed more anxious to peel himself off Marina than she was to relinquish her grip. She grinned at me. Her young admirer stared at the floor.

To my mind, that settled one issue. Obviously, Marina was involved in an innocent romance with one of the local *shibab*— "guy" in the Kuwaiti parlance. And that was a fixable situation, at least as fixable as any problem could be when you were dealing with a couple of sixteen-year-olds. I figured that in this case, between me and Serge, we could run the kid off and get Marina settled down, maybe hormone shots or something.

Visions of using KGB heavies floated across my mind; you know, have a couple of them slam the kid against a wall, draw a little blood, and scare the living hell out of him. They wouldn't even have to talk, just grunt Slavicly. Then, I remembered that Serge was trying to keep his people out of it. Maybe I could get Fitzy to lean on the kid. Fitzy might actually do it out of jealousy; I'd seen the looks he gave Marina. Great, I thought, you'll liberate Marina from the *shibab* to condemn her to Fitzy. What a tremendous favor! So, I stepped off the elevator in front of my apartment door, convinced I knew Marina's great mystery, but at a loss as to how to deal with it.

But once I got in the door, all thoughts of the fair-haired Marina faded. Kirby was home.

He sat on the couch, a half-eaten bowl of rice and chicken on the coffee table in front of him, grains of saffron-yellowed rice clinging to the ends of his mustache. Kirby hated rice and chicken. But it was the cheapest easily available hot meal in Kuwait.

"I've been waiting for you," he began without preamble.

"Kirby, please. You whined at me all day," I said, dumping my briefcase on the floor.

"I find your lack of respect insulting."

"I find your lack of intelligence incomprehensible." I guess I barked at him, because Kirby paused, which was reason to call CNN for a special report. Finally, after his face turned a couple of shades of frustrated red, he stammered out, "What can I do to get you to stay home tonight so Darla—"

"—Debbie—"

"—whatever, will tell me what I need to know?"

"Are you really asking, Kirby?" This was something new indeed. The nightmare roommate was actually showing a little diplomacy. It was, I don't know, so at variance with the Kirby Benson I'd come to hate over the last ten days.

He simply nodded. Two or three of the rice grains loosened their hold and fell to the carpet.

I sank into a flowered chair. "Look, Kirby. What the hell are you into?"

This time Kirby didn't jerk back in indignation; he didn't recoil in self-defense. He just scrunched lower in the chair and knotted his eyebrows together. "This is a sensitive thing, Duffy. I've worked long and hard on this story."

"I understand that, Kirby. But if you want me to run interference with Miss Gonorrhea 1997, you're gonna have to give me a good reason."

The sense of that seemed to sink in, because, finally, his chest heaved a couple of times and he began. "It's like this, see. I was in London, hanging out between jobs. Anyway, I got drunk with this Brit, army guy, who was down here during the Gulf War. He started telling me about all his aches and pains because of the war, you know, the Gulf War Syndrome stuff."

"I thought they proved the Gulf War stuff was bullshit." I'd heard about the symptoms vets were claiming—hair loss, swollen limbs, fatigue, tumors. But nobody had ever pinned down the cause. I think the U.S. and England claimed there *was* no common cause.

"Would you let me finish?"

"Okay."

"Well, finally, toward the end of it—you know this story about swollen ankles, no energy, the rest of it—he said that he didn't dare tell the army doctors that he'd served in the Gulf. I asked him why. 'Because,' he said, 'they won't treat you. They'll walk away from you.' Didn't make any sense to me, so I said, 'Why?' The guy looked at me like I was crazy. 'Because,' he said again, 'you Yanks and us Brits caused the damned thing.'"

Kirby held a hand up as I started to protest. "I know, I know. I thought the same thing. But I came back down here on this teaching assignment and started digging. I've got evidence now, Duffy. Real, honest-to-God evidence."

"You've got a screw loose, Kirby. A real, honest-to-God screw loose. What kind of evidence do you have about Gulf War Syndrome? I'm not trying to rain on your parade here, but, Jesus, what are you saying?"

He settled down then, running his hand through his mangled hair before answering. "I've got proof that the U.S. and England weren't responsible."

"You had me worried there for a second."

"The syndrome was the result of an accident at a secret facility where Kuwait was involved in its own chemical weapons program. During the liberation operation, it got blown up by mistake. The winds shifted the resulting deadly cloud out across the desert. The U.S. and U.K. are covering it up. Bush started the cover-up. Clinton perpetuated it because it was necessary to keep public support for Kuwait high since Saddam Hussein still posed a threat." Kirby stood and paced around the living room. "Okay. That's it. My life's work! Laid bare at your feet!"

"And where's your evidence from? Whores like Debbie? The little Bangladeshi in orange coveralls?"

"I've got other witnesses."

"Yeah, that's right. The secretive Abdulmohsen!"

Kirby stopped and slammed his hands into his ample hips. "All right. I know I'm strange. I know I'm eccentric. But for your information, Abdulmohsen is a former member of the National Assembly and a very respected politician here."

Then I knew where I'd seen the guy's face before—on the cover of the *Arab Times*, as spokesman for the most conservative, Iranian-backed, antigovernment coalition in Kuwait. "Of course, Abdulmohsen is going to feed you a pile of it, Kirby. He hates the present government. Expose a secret chemical weapons program and the government crashes down, to be replaced by Abdulmohsen and his pals with their own secret weapons program. They're using you, Kirby. And besides, how does the unforgettable Debbie fit into this?"

Kirby hung his head. "I'm not sure yet." And when he heard me harrumph, his chin snapped back up. "That's why I need you to talk to her."

"You want me to go on a fishing expedition with a woman who fairly oozes AIDS?"

"Sometimes, Duffy," Kirby began patiently, his hog jowls trembling with the effort, "we have to look beyond ourselves, to loftier goals. Sometimes we have to be willing to make the ultimate sacrifice."

I nodded solemnly. "You've given me a lot to think about, Kirby." And I retreated to my room as fast as my feet would carry me, with Kirby's feet right behind me.

"C'mon, Duffy!" his plaintive voice wailed. "You have to."

"The only things I have to do," I yelled as I bolted my door shut, "are pay taxes and die of this God-awful hangover; okay, well, all I have to do is die."

"See," the muffled voice invaded every crack and seam in the door. "Now you're getting the idea."

You know it's a bad day when Kirby Benson gets the best of you in a verbal duel.

"Never underestimate the power of paranoid-schizophrenics, Duffy," Karen warned me when I called her fourteen Panadol later.

"You're not saying he's onto something, are you?" The idea that Kirby had uncovered a real scoop was, to say the least, as startling as a revelation that Bill Clinton was celibate.

"No, of course not," she scoffed. "But weirdos like Kirby often convince themselves that these conspiracies are true. My advice is to stay away from him."

"I live with him."

"We all have burdens to bear, Duffy. How was the orgy?" The change of subject brought a bitter north wind to her tone.

"You mean the party?"

"Same thing." Same chill.

"It was okay. I don't really remember too much after you left," I admitted.

"And no nasty reminders afterward?"

"Yeah, one hell of a hangover."

"I was thinking of something else," she said.

"Huh?" My head was killing me, and I was having a hard time translating her English.

"You know, those little bugs they warned us about in sex education."

"I got drunk with Serge, okay? That's all. Just drunk. And not really that drunk." I was more than a little testy. "If all you're going to do is accuse me of stuff I didn't do, we can end this conversation now. If I want that, I can call my ex-wife."

"Oohh!" she crooned. "We *are* getting closer. You're already comparing me to the ex. Okay. I'll back off. What are you doing tonight?"

Marina's lovely form bounced into my mind. What the hell? I thought. It might be fun. "Well, in the throes of vodka last nght, Serge confessed to me that his daughter was acting weird, going out at all hours, staying out pretty much all night. You know, normal teenage activities. Anyway, Fitzy told him I'd been a cop, so he decided I was the perfect person to handle the situation. You know, follow her. See what she's up to. Why don't you come with me?"

My humble suggestion was met with a booming silence.

CHAPTER
NINE

"Hello! Anybody out there?" I banged the receiver on the nightstand.

"I don't think that's a very smart idea." Karen's tone left no doubt.

"Jesus, I'm not suggesting political assassination. I'm talking about helping a guy out with a troublesome teenager."

"You're talking about following the daughter of the consul of the Federation of Russian Republics, one of our allies I might add . . ."

"Since when are the Russians our allies?" I slammed in as she paused to breathe.

"The Cold War is over, Duffy, or don't you read the newspapers? And I'm really busy right now. Let me call you back."

"You promise?" Old Man Rejection reared his ugly head.

"Yes, I promise." I replaced the receiver and collapsed on the bed.

"Duffy! You can't get away from me!" The melodious tones of Kirby Benson infested every crack in the door like Tennessee cockroaches.

The phone rang about 9 P.M. Kirby had stopped beating on the door about two hours before. An hour after that I heard the front door slam. The phone rang again. Could it be Karen? Maybe. My hand reached for it. But what if it wasn't? I pulled my hand back.

It rang again. I grabbed the receiver. "Yeah?"

"Duffmannnnn!"

I nearly stroked out; it was Frank Crawford, the Boss.

"What the fucking shit are you up to? Get your stupid, fucking ass up here, man. Staff meeting time. Climb off that faggot Benson and let's go!"

This day reminded me of something Perry Howell told me the day after Jufain tried to kill him "Kuwait, Duffy, can't be measured by normal standards; it must be experienced."

Who would have believed it? A gem of wisdom from the ever-oral Perry. I crawled off the bed and headed for the elevator.

"Duffmannnnnnnnn! Get your ass in here!"

A couple more sheets to the wind and Frank could sail back to the U.S. as a full-rigged schooner. He did that backward stagger-step, a glass of wine in hand, and fell onto the couch, carefully balancing the glass. His spare frame was so light it barely made a dent in the couch.

Perry sat in a chair, a frown burned into his face. Fitzy fiddled with the stereo against the wall, and, just as I feared, the Red Hot Chili Peppers greeted me again.

"What's up, Frank? How's the strep throat?"

I got a cold stare.

"What fucking strep throat?"

"That's what we told Nasser," Perry said calmly.

"Why the fuck did you tell him that?"

"Did you want us to tell him you were smoking hashish and drinking ethanol?"

Frank turned away, tried to drink some wine, but the couch got the benefit instead. "Why the fuck tell the little bastard anything?"

Fitzy, Perry, and I exchanged looks.

"Well, fuck Nasser. Fuck all of you. Anyway, I'm going to Luxor to get some Valium. Tired of all this shit. If you got to tell the fucking Kuwaitis anything, tell 'em, tell 'em, shit, tell 'em whatever the fuck you want to."

"How about a recruiting trip?" I suggested.

Frank sat erect, sending more wine onto the couch. "Great fucking idea, Duffmannnn! Brilliant! Now I know why we hired you." He jabbed his finger at Perry. "You fucking tell Nasser I'm in Luxor trying to hire some real teachers. Fitzy! Turn those goddamned chili-eating bastards off!" Frank jerked to his feet, waving the glass. "Now, we're cooking, goddamnit! Duffmannn! You're one brilliant son of a bitch." Perry and Fitzy pretty much ignored him.

"Hey, Frank. Nasser's really worried about the number of guys we're graduating. Says we've got to start turning out more or we're going to lose the contract."

The scarecrow stopped in his gyrations and swiveled around, sending yet another slap of his wine to water the carpet. "You a smart-ass, Duffman?"

"What?" I was only trying to be responsible. I shifted gears. "No, man. I'm just trying to tell you that we've got to figure out how to chill Nasser out."

Frank smiled at the wall. "Good man. Now, you're with the fucking program."

Fitzy nodded approvingly. Perry looked at me, but it was with neither approval nor even humor. Yeah, Perry, for the first time, looked at me with respect.

"Tell those fucking Arabs that if they'd get their shit together and get those shitheads in class and doing their homework, they'd finish sooner. Don't let them get the upper hand, goddamnit! For every accusation they throw at you, throw five back at them. I've worked on fifteen contracts in ten years, and that's how you do it! Goddamnit!"

"You tell 'em, Frank!" Fitzy said, slipping back to the stereo and cranking up the Chili Peppers again.

"Okay, okay, okay, okay." Frank retreated in his bowlegged stagger-step to the buffet where assorted mineral water bottles filled with wine and ethanol rested. He tried to set his glass down, but, damn it, a bottle was in his way. So, he tossed the glass to the other hand, but that didn't work either and the glass sailed across the room, shattering with a splat on the wall. "Fuck it." Frank abandoned pretense and grabbed one of the water bottles. "Okay, okay, okay, okay, okay—"

When all else fails, I thought, go to the source. Less chance for spillage that way.

"Uh, Frank," I interrupted. "When are you leaving for Egypt?"

He paused for a minute and scratched the thin hair on his chest through his wine-stained tee shirt—actually there were other, mysterious-looking stains, but I didn't want to explore their origins. "Fuck! I'm not sure, maybe on Wednesday. But, shit! What day is it?"

"Tuesday."

Frank nodded. "Yeah. Wednesday. Tomorrow. Shit!" He stopped and yanked his tee shirt off, squeezing the bottle through one of the sleeves. "Fitzy!"

"Yo, Boss!"

"Catch!" And Frank tossed the shirt to Fitzy. "Put that in the sink and run some water over it. Can't fucking go to Luxor without clean clothes."

Once downstairs, I realized that there was little hope for our project or Frank's liver. If either one made it a full year, I'd be one surprised hillbilly. Pouring myself a glass of milk, attractively packaged under the name "laban," I considered all my alternatives, found none with any hope of success, and poured the milk down the sink. Why concentrate on being healthy when life holds no promise? So I stole some of Kirby's homemade wine.

Just as I was settling back on my bed with a glass of Kirby's juice, the phone rang again. It was pushing 10:30 P.M. Probably, I mused, Frank had decided to bypass Luxor and go straight to Nepal or Burma or wherever the almighty poppy flowers are grown.

"Okay, okay." Christ, I thought. I'm beginning to sound like Frank. Snatching the phone up, I snarled, "What the hell do you want?"

"Gee, did I cause that?" It was Karen.

"No. I'm always cranky this time of day." Any port in a storm of embarrassment.

"I'm beginning to notice that. Listen, I'm sorry for being so hard on you."

"Don't worry about it. I bring it on myself."

"Don't preempt my apology with one of your own. Not everything in the world is your fault, Duffy. Allow the rest of us to make mistakes, too. You didn't do anything to cause my reaction. Okay?"

"Whatever you say, ma'am."

"Good. Look. The marines are having a party tomorrow night. Want to go with me?"

I smiled and set Kirby's wine off to the side. "You name the time and place. I'll be there." Life suddenly became bearable again.

The U.S. Embassy in Kuwait is a new, sprawling compound in the Mishref/Bayan area, south of the main city. Two gates provide access on the north and south sides of the compound. The southern access is the main gate, where dignitaries and visitors enter. For embassy staff and for parties, people use the north gate. I found Karen waiting for me at the entrance.

"Well, you dress down okay when you want to," she teased.

I looked down and checked myself out. Jeans. An American Eagle Outfitter shirt. Belt. Socks (though you couldn't see them). And boots. "Is this inappropriate?"

"No," she shook her head. "It's very appropriate. You just look really good dressed that way. Beats those shirts and ties you normally wear."

"That's the standard uniform at the base, but thank you, ma'am," I said in an exaggerated drawl.

"In the interest of time," Karen answered, slipping her arm into mine, "let's go in before the party's over."

The closest thing to a party at an embassy I'd ever been to was Ned McWherter's victory party when he was elected governor of Tennessee for the second time. This was a party sponsored by the small contingent of U.S. Marines assigned to the embassy. God love 'em, U.S. Marines party my way.

Karen led me through a maze of metal detectors, Filipino security guards, sidewalks, perfectly trimmed lawns, tennis courts, and into a pool area covered by a fiberglass roof. A mass of people lounged around. The sounds of the Spice Girls reverberated off the building as another mass of people ground their bodies against each other on a makeshift dance floor.

Through glass doors to my right, I saw a line three deep at a bar. A sign over the bar read: "Beer 500 Fils. Wine 500 Fils. Drinks (Single Shots Only) 500 Fils. Other Beverages: 150 Fils."

"Excuse me," I said to Karen, gazing out at the barbecue grills fired up and toasting hot dogs. "Do you people actually work here?"

"What do you mean?"

"Well, I don't see a single solitary office anywhere in the vicinity. I understand the necessity of camouflage, but does the pool convert into the ambassador's office?"

"You better be glad he's out of town," Karen half-whispered, half-shouted as the Spice Girls explained in detail how to be their lovers. "He's got incredible ears. Actually," she said after a second, "you'd probably get along with him pretty well. He comes from your neck of the woods."

"Yeah?"

"Greetings, mates!" A booming voice exploded and a huge, broad-shouldered man with a ruddy face, close-cut hair, and a "don't fuck with me" look was kissing Karen.

I stuck my hand out. "Ed Duffy. But just call me Duffy before you kiss me."

"Brian O'Neill, of Her Majesty's Armed Forces." The giant engulfed my hand in his EEE version.

Karen smiled at both of us. "Brian's with the military attaché's office at the British Embassy. He shows up at these things to harass Americans."

"Funny," I replied with a wink at O'Neill. "I came to Kuwait to harass American diplomats. I guess that makes us cousins."

"Absolutely," Brian agreed. "C'mon, mate. I'll stand you to some of this Yankee piss-water."

I looked at Karen. "Go ahead. Brian's basically harmless as long as you don't try to match him beer for beer. I need to see my section head."

Brian's large paw fell on my shoulder and using him as blocking back, we plunged into the bar and squirmed into line. "What are you doing in Kuwait?" Brian shouted.

"Teaching English with the Patriot missile project. We do basic English here and then ship them over to the U.S. for advanced English and their actual training on the Patriots." Saying that with a straight face was nearly impossible.

Brian simply nodded. "So," he began after a second, "I'm guessing that they're just as thick over in the air force as they are in the ground forces?"

"Let's put it this way. The English language will never be the same."

"Cheers, mate." We clinked Budweiser cans and turned them up.

"So," I said, "what do you do?"

"Nothing. I sit in an office all day and do nothing. Every once in a while, I get out and check on the British Warrior training. They bought almost three hundred of the lads from us. I'd rather invade Iran single-handed than sit at a desk." He shook his head with disgust.

"Were you out here during the war?"

A mask rolled over his face "You might say that."

"So, the Kuwaiti boys have any more chance of learning how to operate the Warriors than they do the Patriots?"

Brian grinned at that, an infectious, Irish grin. "Not in the bloody least. It's the level of lad they send to us, as I guess it is with you. We get the bottom rung of the ladder. Mostly Bedouins, maybe a couple of years of formal education. Good lads, but with no foundation behind them. It's the concepts, you see, the basic concepts that they're lacking."

"Yeah, I've only been here about ten days, and I see the same thing."

"Yeah," he echoed, "at least you had a choice. With me it was the frigging Ministry of Defense orders. Given a choice between coming to Kuwait and getting an enema, I think I'd take the enema." Brian shook his head in disgust, then stowed the attitude away and brightened.

"Listen, mate, we have a poker game every Wednesday night, if you're interested. You'd fit in with the other lads."

"Sure, just let me know where to go."

Before he could answer, a man with specks of gray dotting his hair approached us from the pool area. I heard a soft, "Oh, shit!" from Brian O'Neill.

The newcomer's hand was out grabbing mine almost before he got within reach. "Hi, my name's Harvey Hanks. Don't believe we've met before. Some kind of weather here, don't you think? I mean, it was hot in Florida, but this isn't just hot. I mean, if a three-balled tomcat got this hot, his dick would melt off."

"Hello, Harvey. I didn't know they let you out of your cage for public events," Brian said pleasantly, but I noticed that his smile was painted on.

Harvey took a long drink, smacking his lips like he was in a Budweiser commercial. "Damn that's good. Nothing like good

American beer. Am I right, Brian? Am I right—I didn't get your name."

"Ed Duffy." Name, rank, and serial number.

"Am I right, Ed? Of course, I am. Here," he said with a lascivious grin. "Here's my card."

There was the good old American eagle, clutching arrows in one claw and an olive branch in the other. But this eagle commanded the middle of the card. Each corner held one of the keystone words of the United States—Dependable, Trustworthy, Honest, Loyal. Above the eagle was the legend, "WE ARE THE **AMERICANS**." Beneath it read the comforting words, "YOU CAN DEPEND ON US. WE DON'T FUCK AROUND."

Then, old Harvey jammed another card into my hand, this one a legitimate embassy card. It read simply, "Harvey Hanks, First Secretary."

"So, what do *you* do here, Harvey?"

Hanks almost blushed. "Awwh, just the old diplomatic grind. What about you?"

"I'm Saddam Hussein's illegitimate son, seeking a return to my rightful place at his side. Hey, there's my date." Karen stood in the door waving. "See you later, Harvey. Brian, give me a call."

If looks could kill, then I took an AK-47 round from Brian's eyes. Harvey, on the other hand, simply looked dumbfounded.

When I finally made it through the crowd to Karen's side, she said, "Now, that's more like it. You're supposed to come running when I call."

"Don't get used to it. I was just escaping from some guy named Harvey Hanks."

Karen's face flushed red. "Where?"

I pointed toward Brian back against the far wall, but Brian and Hanks were gone. "Well, they *were* right there."

"Don't mind Harvey," Karen began. "He's just a little much to take the first time. You'll learn to appreciate his sense of humor."

"Not if it means spending more time with him. He's not your section head or something?"

"No. My section head is fifty going on ninety and avoids parties like the plague. During *Ramadan*, when the ambassador goes out to make calls on all the *diwaniyas*, he's lucky to get my boss to sign up for one night. Why he showed up tonight is beyond me."

"What's a *diwaniya*?"

"A bunch of men getting together to talk about anything and everything. Sort of an Arab smoker. All male, of course, ranging from the very formal to the very informal. During the holy month of *Ramadan*, it's at the top of the very formal scale, and the ambassador makes his ritual rounds." She leaned back against the wall and sipped her drink a little, staring steadily out at the writhing, sweating mass on the dance floor. "Hey, let's go get lost out there."

My Bud was almost empty, so I grabbed Karen's hand. "Your wish is my command."

"Hold that thought for later." She giggled, and, at the risk of boring you further, let's just say that Karen quit acting like a diplomat for a couple of hours, and I began to feel slightly normal. It was a good feeling, one that I realized I'd been yearning for. Suddenly, Kuwait started to be okay again. At least that's what I was thinking as we snuggled up close at her townhouse. Unfortunately, I've never been known for sterling gut feelings.

<hr />

"Trouble coming at twelve o'clock," Fitzy warned me the next day as we wandered down the hall, checking on the classes.

I looked through the glass doors and saw Major Nasser, the Patriot battalion commander. Fitzy and I exchanged glances and backpedaled to the office, snatching Perry on the way.

We arranged ourselves on one side of the conference table, trying our best to look imposing. Sure enough Nasser and his boss burst through the door, shoving George out of the way. Nasser looked around.

"Where's Frank?"

"Luxor," Perry offered. "A recruiting trip."

"Fast recovery from strep throat," Nasser replied, a jaundiced look on his face.

"The miracles of modern medicine." Perry's voice held just a modicum of civility.

"Okay, okay," Nasser interrupted. "We've got a big problem here, guys. The results just came back on the last ECL, and about thirty passed it. You know and I know that that's about 80 percent more than have ever passed it before. Now, the U.S. Embassy is claiming that we cheated, that we got our hands on the answers. You guys are going to help us out. You guys are going to assure the embassy that we did not have access to the answers."

Fitzy and I froze. Perry stood and smiled at the four of us. "If I'd known this was about testing, I would have stayed at my desk. Testing is their responsibility," and he nodded to us. "I have other work to do."

Yeah, I thought, like scoring on the Bangladeshi teaboy. "Of course, gentlemen, Fitzy and I will be glad to tell the embassy that they're mistaken." I caught a sharp, pointed glare from Fitzy out of the corner of my eye, but, I mean, here was Nasser, holder of my fate, demanding a favor, if you can demand a favor.

The colonel and Nasser looked at each other, and Nasser nodded. "Good. Remember this, guys," Nasser said to both of us, but he was staring at me, "we're in this together." They rose and left without another word.

"Jesus, Duffy!" Fitzy's face was apple red. "Why'd you tell them that?"

"What else was I going to tell them? Frank's not here. Perry's blown us off, so to speak. If you haven't noticed, it's just me and you and the Kuwaiti Air Force."

"Frank *did* give them the answers." Fitzy sat down with a thud and hung his head in his hands. "The last time a sergeant came over from the embassy to administer the test, Frank slipped the answer keys out of his briefcase and copied them. He figured nobody would be the wiser, and we could get some of these guys out of our hair."

I had to grab a chair for balance. It wasn't every day that I promised to go head-to-head with the U.S. Embassy in defense of the Kuwaiti Air Force for a "crime" it had been a party to. And if I didn't defend the air force, Nasser would make sure I stayed in Kuwait for the next millennium.

"Hey, boss!"

I looked up at little George standing in the doorway with a foolish grin on his face. "What?" Nothing George could say could possibly be any worse.

"Where Mr. Kirby?"

This was a distraction I didn't want or need. "Check his classroom."

"Come, boss." George urged me out.

"Not now, George. Later."

"No, boss. Come now."

I left Fitzy moaning and went into the corridor where I found twelve smiling Kuwaiti faces. "Yeah? Why aren't you guys in class?"

"*Mafi* teacher, Mister," one offered.

"Mr. Kirby, *mo' mahjoud*," another one chimed in.

"What do you mean '*mafi* teacher'?" I turned to George.

"'No teacher.' Mr. Kirby, he not in class."

"Well, go find him. He's probably in the latrine."

The guys shook their heads and one of them rattled something off in Arabic to George. "They say he not here all morning."

"And they're just now telling us?" My watch said 10:30, three and a half hours of class gone. But, then, I put myself in their shoes and imagined an entire day with Kirby Benson.

Sticking my head back into the office, I yelled at Fitzy. "C'mon, Fitz, Benson's missing in action. Let's see if we can find him."

But twenty minutes later, I began to realize that things were going from worse to . . . whatever comes after worse. Not only was Kirby nowhere to be found, but none of the other teachers remembered having seen him that day. And as I thought back to the early morning, I hadn't seen him in the apartment either. In fact, the last time I'd seen him had been two nights before, right before Frank had called the impromptu staff meeting.

"Any suggestions?" I turned to my faithful Irish companion.

Fitzy scratched his curly hair. "Why don't you go back to the apartments and see if the old fart croaked in his bed or something? I'll keep things in the road here."

"Grand idea." At least I could avoid the Patriot Cafeteria and its alleged food.

━◆━

Mohammed Al-Zaki was a tall, urbane Egyptian, with closely cropped, nappy black hair and an American accent straight out of Poughkeepsie, New York, where he had once managed a Kentucky Fried Chicken. But Mohammed left his fast-food career behind for the fascinations of running an apartment complex in Kuwait.

My only contact with Zaki had been a simple introduction by Fitzy my first day in Kuwait. He seemed nice enough, though I heard Frank refer to him once as "a spineless, bootlicking toady." I mean, anybody that Frank didn't like must have some major redeeming qualities.

As I sped into the parking space in my new Galant, courtesy of the departed Fuzzball, I checked the office and sure enough Zaki was sitting behind the desk banging away on a calculator.

"Oh, Mr. Duffy, sir! How are you? It has been so long since you came to visit!"

Funny, I thought, I couldn't remember *ever* having come to visit. Maybe Frank was right. "Great to see you, too, Mohammed. Listen, have you seen Mr. Kirby today?" I leaned on the door frame and caught my breath.

Mohammed's eyebrows knitted together. "Nooo, Mr. Duffy. I think maybe," he paused for a second, that same look of grave concern wrinkling his face, "I think maybe, Farouq told me that Mr. Kirby left late last night with some Kuwaiti gentlemen. But he didn't come back."

That gave me something to chew on. First, that meant Kirby might really be missing, and, second, it meant that Mohammed's watchful eyes saw a hell of a lot; something I'd need to keep in mind for the future. I thanked him and headed up to the apartment.

A few minutes later, standing outside Kirby's door, I hesitated. Never before had I invaded the sanctum sanctorum of the Great Writer, and I can't say the idea turned me on. Something about Kirby Benson called up a combination of that lustrous odor of sour milk and the smoky remnants of a fire in a cigar factory. Sort of the way the garden smelled after Daddy made me cover it in manure. And that's exactly how Kirby Benson's room reeked when I twisted the doorknob and entered. My greatest fear was that he was dead in his bed.

The room, beyond the smell, needed disaster relief. Dirty clothes covered the carpet. The sheets were an odd brown color, but they seemed to have the same design as my own white sheets. The parts of the floor that weren't decorated with clothes were covered in sheets of paper. Two ashtrays overflowed on the nightstand, cigarette butts lying across each other like a load of logs.

But the desk was different. Too different. An old typewriter sat in the middle. But no papers were on the desk. No ashtray. It was almost ludicrously clean. I checked the typewriter and even the ribbon was missing. My stomach bottomed out. Something was wrong with this picture. Kirby Benson really was missing.

CHAPTER
TEN

I called out to the base, but Goanese George mumbled that Fitzy had gone somewhere. "Who's in charge?" I asked.

George just giggled and hung up.

I thought about calling Karen, but what could she do? If Kirby really was in some kind of trouble, the embassy would demand more proof than just a missing typewriter ribbon. And given Kirby's erratic behavior, they'd probably suggest that he took a hike on his own. Finally, they would pass the buck to the Kuwaiti police. According to my watch, it was about 1:30, almost time to leave work anyway. I kicked off my shoes and settled on the couch.

The funny thing was, I came to Kuwait to escape stress and life's little complications. Now, I was discovering that anxiety had trailed me six or seven thousand miles. I'd be safer in Detroit. Somehow or other, despite all the rampaging thoughts flickering through my gray cells, I fell asleep.

BAM! BAM! BAM! The decibels came as close to busting my eardrums as the battering ram came to shattering my door.

"All right!" I said, climbing up from the couch, and then the lock gave, splintering the wood around it and a crazed Russian bull stormed into the room.

"I'll kill her! I'll kill her! Do you hear me! I'll kill her!" Serge grabbed me around the throat and squeezed, for effect I suppose, but the end result was that I started to lose consciousness.

"Serge!" I spluttered as the room faded to black. "Let me go!"

He looked at me then, noticing, I guess, that my eyeballs were bulging.

"Marina! She not come back last night. No! All night, she stayed out! You must to help me, Duffy! I cannot live like this. I must know what she is doing! Help me, Duffy! Help me!" And he grabbed my shoulders, shaking me like a leaf. My head bounced like a dashboard ornament. Boing! Boing! Boing!

"Ser-r-r-ge! St-o-o-p-p-p-p i-i-i-t!" But he didn't, so I slammed a wobbly fist into his solar plexus. His stomach had the consistency of a giant marshmallow, and my fist disappeared into a lifetime of vodka, herring, and caviar.

Serge fell back under the shot, his anger disappearing. He slumped onto my couch and his arms flopped down between his legs. He dropped his big head. "Duffy. I cannot sleep for three nights now." The plea came out in a whisper, just a breath of air.

I decided to try one more time to extricate myself. "The other day, I was on the elevator and there was Marina and some Arab kid ramming their tongues down each other's throats. Maybe she was out with him."

He waved a hand like I'd just said the stupidest thing in the world. "That is only Ibrahim. He—how you say—couldn't find his . . . dick . . . yes, dick, with both hands. This is different. His parents make him come home by eleven. No, this is something else, something different." And he grabbed my hands. "I am begging you. Find out what Marina is doing. You are my only hope."

I gave up. "Okay. Okay. Tonight, as soon as she leaves, call me." Unfortunately, I never learned to keep my mouth shut, hence my ability to insert foot at every conceivable opportunity. My mother used to say it was inherited. My father said it was just stupidity.

Even as I was musing about my genetic failings, Serge reached into his coat and pulled out a bottle of Stolichnaya to seal the deal. "Look, Serge. If I'm going to follow Marina tonight, I need a clear head. Okay?"

"Of course," he said with a smile. "Nothing clears your head like wodka. Ask any doctor."

I watched Serge drink for probably two hours, but I just couldn't survive another drunk. I kept my glass full of water, and every time he went to fill it up, I'd show him it was full. He never caught on. Finally, I shoved him out the door, confident that he was too drunk to call me when Marina went out. As for me, I fell asleep again. I'd forgotten all about Kirby, and that was the best part of the whole affair. I could conveniently forget about Frank, the Patriot project, Karen, and surrender myself to blissful catatonia.

At least until the phone rang.

"Hey, Duffy! What's happening?" Fitzy.

"I'm dying."

"Did you find Benson?" He sounded altogether too happy.

"No. I tried to call you at work, but George said you'd taken off somewhere."

"We ran out of staples, so I went to get some."

I hung up, ready for another few hours of uninterrupted sleep.

Until the phone rang again.

"Duffy! Where are you?" That Slavic accent. It was Serge, still drunk, still obsessed with his daughter's waywardness. "She left, just one minute before I call you."

"Okay, okay. Jesus, Serge, I'm still drunk." Okay. I lied. But it was worth a shot.

"Better. You will not be afraid. Hurry! Hurry!"

Praying that I'd be too late, I eased the Galant out of the lot and rolled down toward the end of the building. And there she was: sweet, blond, incredibly stacked Marina, wearing a black leather miniskirt sewn to her body and a red top that left nothing to the imagination but the exact circumference of her nipples. She stood at the end of the main entrance, glancing nervously at her watch. Obviously, she was waiting for somebody; I figured Ibrahim. It had been my experience that teenagers always know more than you give them credit for. And I was betting that Ibrahim knew exactly where to find his genitalia and what to do with it.

Imagine my surprise when a taxi pulled up and Marina hopped in, checking over her shoulder in case she was being followed, which she was, but she was looking for her father on foot, not me in a Galant. I kicked it into gear and took off after them.

Kuwaiti cabbies are usually non-Kuwaiti Arabs—Egyptians, Jordanians, Syrians, Palestinians, a few Pakistanis thrown in on the side. To watch them drive, you'd think they ordered their driver's licenses through We Forge 'Em, You Gorge 'Em, Inc. The licenses look like the real thing, but they don't have any bearing on the possessor's ability to drive. I was torn between wondering whether this phenomenon was born here and spread to New York, Philadephia, and so on, or vice versa. But what I didn't understand, until we hit the the roundabout at the beginning of 5th Ring Road, was that *everybody* in Kuwait drove that way.

Horns blared in my ear. Caprices, BMWs, Mercedes all crowded me. I got something resembling the finger from a half-dozen Arab maidens, faces and heads covered, one gloved hand gesturing at me while the other pressed a cell phone to her ear. Maybe a dog was steering.

While Kuwaitis drive on the right side of the road, they have adopted most other British traffic staples, like roundabouts instead of traffic lights. Rather than keep traffic moving, they create jam-packed circles of cars, bumper-to-bumper, all inching forward, forcing themselves into spaces I wouldn't try to put my pinkie in, all trying to get somewhere before somebody else. For no real reason, you understand, just to get there first. And right in the center of the circle is always some kind of homage to one sheikh or another, always impeccably dressed in *ghoutra* (headdress) and sunglasses. Somehow, regardless of who it is, he always looks exactly like Alec Guinness in *Lawrence of Arabia*.

But I managed to keep the taxi in view, about four cars ahead of me, making the turn onto 5th Ring. And that's when I almost lost them. The driver saw a break and gunned it, zipping between two aged Suzukis, and barreling down 5th Ring Road like a Scud out of Baghdad.

Not to be outdone, I forced a Nissan truck carrying a camel in the bed against the curb and slithered off the roundabout, hot on the trail of the taxi.

Once on the ring road, it was smooth sailing. I stayed a couple of cars back, and the taxi driver headed out further, away from the city, until we got to the exit for Jabriya, and then he swerved off at the last second, leaving me two lanes out. But I'd already been in Kuwait long enough to know how to tackle that problem. I jumped the curb, bounced over speed bumps, and cut off two other cars jousting for the one available lane. Still, the taxi driver and Marina were oblivious. Just another night on the Kuwaiti freeway.

On they went, winding through the backstreets of Jabriya, dodging the occasional citizen who ventured into their path, up through embassy row, past the Pakistani, Philippine, and Japanese missions. I began wondering if they were headed over to Surra, the next suburb to the west, but then, just as I settled into a comfortable pace, the cabbie spun onto yet another street.

I wrestled the Galant into the turn and kept my distance. At least until the taxi slid into a U-turn and started back up the opposite direction. All Kuwaiti streets of any significance have five-inch-high medians with legal U-turns cut into the medians, and it was into one of those that the cabbie swerved, as I shot down the street past it.

Shit! It was the only word I could come up with. About a quarter mile down the street, I saw another U-turn and I pushed the Galant into it, trying all the while to keep an eye on the taxi in my rearview mirror. And just as I rounded the turn, I saw the taxi veer off and head toward 4th Ring Road.

No problem, I thought. I kept thinking that when I saw the taxi stop in front of an aerobics studio. Great! Marina's big secret was that she took aerobics late at night. I drove past, making another U-turn in front of a Bint al Deek, sort of Kuwait's answer to Kentucky Fried Chicken, and parked in a narrow parking lot across the street from the studio.

The local guys were zipping in and out, picking up chicken and rice take-out and ogling the girls across the street. I never learned what Bint al Deek means. Bint means girl. Al means "of." Girl of Deek. Sounds like a strange name for a chicken restaurant. But my car blended in, and it made sense just to wait Marina out. That way, I told myself, I could always tell Serge that I left no stone unturned. What I didn't expect was for her to just stand outside the studio, fidgeting, sidestepping, obviously waiting for something else to happen.

And then something did.

A shadow fell across my window, and a pair of hands started pawing at the glass.

CHAPTER
ELEVEN

I shrank away from the window as another shadow filled the windshield.

"*Shinoo t'abee?*" came a muffled cry.

What in the hell?

"Mister! Mister!"

It was Bint al Deek's curbside service. Replete with robed Egyptian teenagers, all clamoring at the window for my order.

I rolled the window down, craning my head around the fidgeting shadows for Marina. "Mister! *Shinoo t'abee?* What you want?" One of the shadows pushed the window down and stuck his head in the car.

I pushed back, a little too hard, sending him stumbling back, and the other two laughed at him. "*Mafi!*" I answered. Nothing.

"But, Mister!"

"*Mafi!*"

"Why you here?"

I ignored the question.

The next thing I heard was the drumlike repetition of hands slapping my car. *"Yella!"* the Egyptian commanded angrily. Obviously, since I wasn't a paying customer, I needed to move. And when they finally backed away from the car, I saw that there really was no reason to hang around.

Marina was gone.

—◆—

"What did you expect, Duffy?" Karen was not sympathetic. It was about midnight, and, apparently, she'd been trying to call me for a couple of hours. I hadn't been anxious to get home anyway, figuring that Serge would be lying in wait and that this time, he would clamp those ham-sized hands around my esophagus for good.

"Nothing. I mean, well . . . uh, hell, I don't know."

"Exactly," she answered smugly, and I considered slamming the phone against the wall. "My advice is to tell Sergei to do his own dirty work."

"Jesus, Karen. It's his daughter. We're not talking about going out and doing a KGB hit for him."

She sighed. God, I loved it when she sighed. It was like a combination of Julia Roberts and Sophie Marceau. "No, Duffy, we're talking about helping an alcoholic, diplomatic outcast handle his domestic affairs. That spells trouble in any protocol book."

"Don't forget, sweetheart. I'm not a diplomat. I don't have a protocol book."

"No," she remarked acidly. "You are a subcontractor to the United States government, however, and you are consorting with an agent of a foreign power. That may not be the definition of espionage, but it smells. I certainly wouldn't want to explain to a congressional committee how I agreed to tail a Russian diplomat's daughter, how I spent half my time drunk in that same Russian's apartment, while all the time I was an employee on a classified government contract."

"Listen, if that was all I had to worry about answering for . . ." I left it hanging there. I wasn't quite ready to tell Karen about the cheating scandal, or the disappearance of Kirby Benson, or Frank's imminent, Valium-induced return. "Let's just say that I feel pretty confident about defending myself against any charges like that."

I checked the clock. Yep, about 12:30 A.M. This was worse than college. At least in college, you could pass out, skip class the next day, and recover. Here, reveille sounded at 5:30 A.M. every day. It was worse than the army. There wasn't a sick call. "Listen. I'm going to hit the sack. Diplomats may party all night, but government contractors are human."

"Well, will I see you tomorrow night?"

Tomorrow night. Seemed like there was something I'd promised somebody . . . Brian. That's right. Tomorrow was Wednesday. And I had promised Brian O'Neill I'd play poker with him. "Can't. I told Brian I'd play cards with him and the lads." I attempted a British accent.

"Well, Thursday night then?"

"Yeah. I'll buy you dinner on Thursday."

"Duffy? Stay away from Sergei and his daughter. I don't want anything to happen to you."

"I'll try." As I heard the phone click, I realized it'd been a long time since anybody had said they cared. I had to come halfway around the world to hear it, but that only made the sound sweeter.

Work the next day was its normal travesty. Kirby Benson was still missing. Frank was still in Luxor; Perry pointed to the possibility of a Valium overdose. We all thought that was for the best. I mean, how many milligrams of Valium can you take on top of rotgut wine, "bug juice" I'd started calling it, or ethanol before you crank off this mortal coil?

And Major Nasser kept giving me dirty looks all day. He wandered through with a sarcastic, "Frank still on that recruiting trip?" comment. George talked in hurried whispers on the phone, and the normal smile on his face disappeared with every call. It struck me that George could be a foreign agent, but then, couldn't everybody?

After work, I avoided Serge, took a quick nap after checking that my roommate was still missing, and then bounced up, clear-headed for the first time in days, and ready to drive to Brian's place in Mansouriya, near the British Embassy. Like the U.S., the Brits tended to put their employees up relatively close to the office.

It was a neat, two-story villa of sandstone brick. The table was set up, cards, chips (to bet), and chips (to eat). Another table against the far wall held a beer drinker's paradise, Foster's, St. Pauli Girl, Beck's, Amstel, Lowenbrau, you name it, all iced down, all ready for waiting stomachs.

"New meat, mates." Four other guys were there—three Brits, including Brian, and a German named Franz. Brian introduced me around and we settled quickly into a game of seven-card stud. When it came to playing poker, I knew how, I wasn't bad, but my daddy taught me long ago that you can lose your shirt in a heartbeat to old cardsharps, and that's what these guys looked like to me, a bunch of old army vets who'd spent every payday for the last fifteen or twenty years taking cash off the less skilled.

It took about five minutes to have them all pegged: Franz was the worst of the lot; his face couldn't hide a thing. Nat, a dapper major in the artillery, had a good face, but his betting tipped his hand. Graham, who didn't offer his branch, was solid both in his face and his betting. But Brian was the best of all. His face drew you in, making you believe you had a chance, and he bet cautiously all the time, never giving you a clue until he had you betting like a madman, convinced you had him on the run. Then, he'd trot out three aces, or a full house, or a straight, and a tiny little smile would stretch the corners of his mouth.

I soaked down three Foster's in the first hour, playing my cards as conservatively as possible, still losing about three or four dollars, but never more than fifty or seventy-five cents a hand. Brian started watching me carefully.

"Ye play ye're cards close to the vest, mate."

"Just don't want to get raped by you guys."

"You're not our type, mate," Nat assured me. "We just want your money."

"What else is there to do?" Brian asked. "Pair of queens bets a quarter."

"You could chase women." I checked Brian's pair of queens, noted that I had nothing even close and folded.

"You're just rubbing it in, mate." Brian turned to the others. "This bloody Yank only hit the country a couple of weeks ago, and he's already nailed down the finest looking *bint* at the U.S. Embassy."

Franz sighed heavily. "Yes. Unless I get, how do you say it, lucky? Unless I get lucky, I may have to visit one of the whorehouses soon. *Grosse Gott!* Never, in all my life, have I had to pay for a woman."

"Whorehouses? In Kuwait? Isn't that against Muslim rules?" I knew I sounded naïve.

Brian laughed. "Most of them are flats run by Filipino whores. Ten dinar a pop, so to speak. We're always having some enlisted lad come in dripping. There's a couple of them here in Mansouriya, a high-class joint out in Farwaniya, but most of them are in Abraq Kheitan. The Kuwaitis don't use them though. Too good to do a Filipino whore. They use a phone number and for a hundred dinar a night, they get a beautiful Lebanese slapper all to themselves."

"Sounds expensive," I said. Right then, a hundred dinar was a fortune; I was still waiting for my first payday.

"Yeah, mate. But the things those girls can do," Nat crowed.

And just about that time, I noticed that I'd lost two dollars on the pot, to Brian. "You're a sleazy poker player, O'Neill. You get me talking about whores and, before I know it, you've jacked up the pot on me."

"That's the way the game's played, mate. Just trying to figure out how to get at you."

"Yeah, well, I'm not sure I'd want to meet you across the battle lines."

"More likely to meet him behind your lines than in front of them," Nat said with a wink, but Graham shot him a dirty look and Brian avoided them both. I made a note of it and anted up for the next round.

Two more Foster's later, another three dollars down the drain, and I finally picked up a pattern in friend Brian. When he was bluffing, he tapped his right index finger on his cards ever so slightly. When he had a solid hand, the finger didn't move at all.

"So," I said, warmed by the beer and my newfound intelligence, "how do you guys know so much about the whorehouses of Kuwait?"

Brian grinned as he dealt the cards, showing himself with a pair of deuces up. "Every once in a while," he answered, dropping fifty cents in the pot, "one of the tea and crumpet gang gets his dick caught in the wrong crack, and one of us gets the joy of pulling him out."

"What's the tea and crumpet gang?" I had a queen showing with another in the hole. Brian added nothing but junk to his own hand, but he continued betting with confidence, and the index finger started tapping.

"The diplomats," Nat answered for him. "They're almighty careful what words come out of their mouths, but they ain't nearly so careful when it comes to plugging in their stick."

"That's the God's truth," Graham interjected.

"Everybody's got problems," I agreed. Now, Brian was still showing only the pair of deuces, but he was betting like he had a third in the hole. Graham had a possible straight. Franz bottomed out after the fifth card and folded. Nat had the makings of an ace high straight, but he was betting cautiously, which told me he hadn't finished it and was seeing how the wind was blowing.

By the seventh and final card, I showed nothing but junk, but two queens lay nestled face down in my hand and a third smiled at the rest of the boys. Keeping a straight face was something of a problem, but I sucked in my gut, pinched myself behind my knee and managed to frown convincingly. Graham and Nat still showed only possibles, nothing concrete.

"Why do I think you've got three of those little deuces hiding over there?" I asked Brian for good measure.

He grinned, still tapping that index finger in a regular rhythm. "You're a suspicious man. I'm in for fifty." He shoved the chips out.

"I'll see it and raise a quarter." That caused his eyebrow to go up.

Graham folded. Nat matched my bet and called, not because he thought he could win, I figured, but because he wanted to see who was bluffing, me or Brian.

Brian's finger did a machine-gun tap dance on the table. His eyes flickered from me to the cards and back to me. Finally, he flipped them all over. "Fold."

I breathed a sigh of relief and showed my three ladies. Brian grinned from ear to ear.

"You scalped me, mate."

I raked in the pot and checked my watch. "Hate to run while I'm on a streak, but I've got things to do tomorrow."

"No problem. Same time next week. You can make this game interesting."

Of course, it was easy for him to laugh. I was still down about five dollars. All of it to him.

＿＿＿

Now I was psyched again. This was a life I could enjoy. A good-looking girlfriend, cool friends from faraway places, adventures every night, beer to drink almost any time I wanted it. Kuwait wasn't half as bad as I had thought it was, and driving the Galant down Gulf Street that night toward Salmiya, I could think of a dozen places worse. As the lights of the Kuwait Towers receded behind me, even thoughts of Kirby Benson and Serge's daughter, Marina, couldn't drag me down off that high. Hell, even the periodic rat-tat-tat of submachine gun fire couldn't spoil my mood. Too bad the high wasn't fated to last.

Back at the hacienda, I wandered in my euphoric haze up the elevator to my apartment. As I rode the creaking, complaining booth, I kept hearing "THUD! THUD! THUD!" from somewhere along the shaft. My euphoria faded a little.

Then I realized the thuds weren't in the shaft, they were on *my* floor.

I started pressing the down button for all I was worth.

Too late.

The door opened and I braced myself.

Serge. Pounding the hell out of my door again, with his blond hair flapping with every slamming hand.

"Serge." I tapped him lightly on the shoulder.

He spun and started a big ham-fisted hand down toward my head, but I met it with my own hand, wrapped tightly around his wrist.

We glowered like that for a few seconds, my hand trembling under the weight and strength of his arm. But one too many years of vodka and cigarettes caught up with him and he re-laxed. "Sorry, Duffy," he said, slouching back against the door, his face sagging with every ounce of loose flesh. "Sometimes, sometimes, I get, how do you say it, carried away, *da*, carried away."

He reached down to grab a brown paper bag sitting next to the door. Wodka.

As we went in I noticed again how quiet the apartment was. Benson had been missing for about forty-eight hours, and sooner or later, I'd have to tell somebody. I could only guess that Fitzy briefed Frank on the way back from the airport.

Serge extricated the bottle from the bag and sidestepped into the kitchen looking for glasses. Weddings, funerals, missing friends, wayward daughters, troubled marriages, all were occasions for drinking when it came to Serge. You really had to admire his focus.

"Drink," he insisted.

How did it go? "Whiskey on beer, have no fear. Beer on whiskey, mighty risky." I'm not sure how vodka fit into it, but I seemed to have them in the right order. So, I turned it up, knowing that to argue with Serge was to simply postpone the inevitable.

"So, Duffy, tell me. What did you find out? A boyfriend? A party? What?" His words sounded insistent, and they came out with more confidence than I expected. Obviously, he *really was* expecting me to figure this thing out.

"Well, the truth is, I sort of lost her. Hell, Serge. I got held up over in Jabriya."

He shook his massive head. I ran it down for him. How I followed the taxi to Jabriya. How the Bint al Deek boys surrounded me. And how when I finally got rid of them, Marina was gone.

"I—I—," Serge's lip started quivering. "I expected too much. *Mumkin*—maybe—I expected too much. But . . ." and he grabbed my hand, pinching the hell out of me, "you will try again."

I winced, pulling my hand away. "Of course, I will."

"Good. Now, we can drink. Where's Fitzy?"

"I don't know," I answered The vodka was spreading out over the Foster's and giving me that warm glow that always precedes a nasty drunk.

"I'll call him."

Somehow, I must have dozed off, passed out, or otherwise lost consciousness, because the next thing I knew, I heard voices. I blinked hard, trying to erase the fog in my eyes. Who was it? They both sounded familiar. One of them sounded like, Kirby? No, that wasn't right. I tried to sit up and couldn't. Good God, I only had two shots. The two voices were getting angry. I could hear the volume and pitch go up, but I couldn't keep my eyes open long enough to see any faces.

Then, something crashed against the wall—something that went "tinkle" when it fell to the floor. I pulled my head far enough off the couch to look at the source of the noise.

It was Fitzy. He'd just bashed the intercom phone and was looking for something else to break. Serge was sitting on the floor, downing vodka, and egging him on.

Pretty soon, Fitzy graduated from bashing telephones to bashing pots and pans on the walls. Didn't have quite the same tonal quality as the Red Hot Chili Peppers, but it was close. Serge just sat on the floor staring down at his bottle, his pudgy fingers playing with the mouth absently.

"You okay, Serge?" He just looked so, I don't know, pitiful.

"Life is not good, Duffy." He shook his mammoth head. "*Walla*. Life is not good."

"We all have problems, Serge." I snatched the bottle and turned it up. What did I care? I was at home and had all the next day to recover. "Yours will work out."

"I don't believe it, Duffy. Sometimes I think about ending it all. Do you have a gun?"

At that particular moment, I didn't really hear Serge clearly; I was watching Fitzy try to walk up the wall.

"Duffy!"

I turned back to Serge. "No, sorry, pal. No gun. Maybe later."

"*Maalesh*. Never mind. I find one somewhere else."

Fitzy was trekking about two-thirds of the way up the wall, then falling back on his butt. Didn't seem to bother him, though. He'd just stand up, take another swig of vodka, and plant his size fourteen shoes on the wall again.

"Let's go! Come on! Come on!" Serge said a second later. He already had his jacket on. That much I could see.

"Go where?"

"To find girls. Come on!"

"Are you serious?" For once Fitzy was making some remote sense. And he collapsed back to the floor.

"I will drive!" announced Serge.

He was the drunkest of the bunch. But, I shrugged, if you've got to die—once again—why not go out with a big bang.

Somehow, either by the will of Allah or some innate homing instinct, we found Serge's car in the basement parking lot, a Galant just like mine. "Where are we going?" I asked again, leaning against the car, fascinated with the little patterns my fingers were making in the dust. Serge stopped and swayed a little. "I don't remember. But, never mind, we'll find it."

Tires screeched. Rubber separated from tire. My stomach cramped. Fitzy's face was turning a compelling shade of green.

"Let's go to the circus." Serge suggested. Apparently all thought of girls had fled.

"What circus?"

"The Italian Circus," he exclaimed. "They have these girls with really big tits. We'll pay them for some fun after the show. *Walla*, I swear it. Anything for my friends."

The car careened around into a U-turn.

Serge tossed something into my lap. By the time I realized that it was a bottle of Stoli, the damage was done and I curled into a ball as visions of my unborn children vanished before my eyes. "Good God, Serge!" I squeaked. "Be careful where you throw that thing."

"Have another drink. *Inta laissem!* You must!"

My stomach rumbled ominously as the liquor hit bottom and mixed with the rest.

"You know, Duffy," Serge said, a strange sort of calm in his voice. I noticed that he checked the rearview to see Fitz passed out. "I hate my wife. *Walla!* I hate her so much. Sometimes I think about killing myself. Do you have a gun, Duffy?"

"Didn't we just have this conversation?" The consul of the Federation of Russian Republics was driving maniacally, drunkenly, through the streets of Kuwait declaring his hatred for his wife and suggesting suicide. "Everybody hates their wife at some point, Serge. You'll feel different sober," I counseled. "I know I do. But, hell, if you hate her that much, divorce her."

"I can't divorce her. I want to divorce her, but I can't."

"Why not? Is it some kind of Russian Orthodox kind of thing?" I tried to focus on the street, but it was passing by too fast. Seemed to me that the cops should be stopping the sidewalk for speeding.

"You don't understand. I am, how do you say it, I am shortlisted. Yes, *da! Da!* Shortlisted for ambassador. I must only finish this tour, and then I go to a special school in Moscow to become an ambassador."

"That's great, Serge. But, why can't you divorce Linna?" Was I missing something in the translation?

"Because," he said. "She is a bitch. And her father is a colonel in the KGB—I mean VCR, or is it FSB, the initials, they change too much in my country. It is impossible." He swerved to avoid a Nissan Gloria. I frowned for a minute. What the hell was a Nissan Gloria? Sounded like a car named after somebody's girlfriend.

"If I divorced the bitch," he continued, "I would lose any chance for ambassador."

"The world's a rough place," I said, opting for reality therapy.

"*Da.*" Serge nodded his head gravely. "Better that we should die than have to face it." And he swerved the car toward an oncoming Mercedes.

"Jesus! Serge! Stop!" But he wasn't listening. I glanced into the backseat, but Fitzy was oblivious, his head tucked down around his knees, his face already past green and turning to black.

"All right. Okay!" said Serge. He twisted the wheel and missed the Mercedes by a hair. I breathed a sigh, until I saw an ugly brown Nissan Cedric crawling along in front of us.

The crash came quickly, mercifully, and we weren't moving very fast. My shoulder slammed into the door as Serge's head bounced off the steering wheel, opening a cut on his forehead that left a thin stream of blood rolling down the side of his face. Behind me, I heard a thunk as Fitzy was hurled against the seat.

"Serge! Are you okay?" Why I was worried about this bastard instead of myself, I'll never know. Oblivious to my inner struggle, Serge raised his head and grinned, the blood reaching down to his chin and dripping onto the steering wheel.

"Are we alive?"

Then, something small and noisy appeared at the window, and little flesh-colored hammers started banging on the glass. A skinny Pakistani was doing a bizarre dance in the street and screaming at the top of his lungs. What was left of his car was stopped in front of us, the rear bumper looking like a crumpled chewing gum wrapper.

The Pakistani stopped in mid-scream and started for me. "You son bitch! You make accident my car!"

By that time, a couple of other cars had stopped, and some robed Kuwaitis were gathering. Two of them tackled the Pakistani.

"You Ameriki?" one of them asked. I nodded.

Serge rolled out of the car and rolled onto the street. I lurched toward him, afraid he was dead. He rose to a half-crouch and fell back down.

"They drunk! They drunk!" The Pakistani kept up his manic dance.

A police car pulled up and two of Kuwait's finest stepped out in their khaki uniforms. The older and thinner of the two walked up to the Pakistani and frowned. "*Shinoo hadha?*" he asked. I already knew what that meant: "What is this?"

"He drunk! He drunk!" The Pakistani danced some more, pointing all the while at Serge who was attempting to resurrect himself from the pavement.

The older cop edged over to Serge, glanced at the golden diplomatic plates on the car, and reached a hand down to help him up. Serge rambled to his feet as Fitzy chose that moment to tumble out of the backseat.

"See! See! They all drunk! Drunk! Drunk! Drunk!"

In a more sober moment, I would have hit the Paki, anything to shut him up. But the Kuwaiti policeman took care of that. A hand blurred, and the sickening crunch of fist against flesh echoed off a nearby building.

"Why you hit me? *They're* drunk!" the Pakistani whined, holding the side of his face.

The policeman glanced one more time at the unmistakable diplomatic plates, sighed and turned back to the Pakistani. "Alcohol is illegal in Kuwait. They cannot be drunk." He assessed Serge. "Sir, did this man make an accident?" He pointed the proverbial finger at the Pakistani. Serge nodded with a sorrowful shake of the head.

The older cop jerked his head at the little fellow. The other policeman strode forward, cuffed the Pakistani and shoved him toward the squad car. "Please follow me to the station so that we can write a proper report."

For a man with about two liters of vodka in him, Serge sobered up fast. He pulled Fitzy to his feet and half pushed, half threw him at me. "Take him home. I'll take care of this. Go. *Yella imchee*. Walk."

The policeman ignored us, so I propelled Fitzy ahead of me, anxious to beat a hasty retreat. Hell, I was retreating faster than Saddam's Republican Guards when Stormin' Norman knocked on the door. Unfortunately, Fitzy sort of stopped after a couple of hesitant steps. His shoulders began to jerk up and roll forward and his hands shook. And there it came, all over the side of the police car, about two dozen shots of vodka, half of a Domino's pizza, and assorted other bodily fluids adding their unique consistency to the police chariot.

Both cops headed toward us, but Serge cut them off at the pass. He jabbered something in Arabic and the cops pulled up short and started laughing.

"What did you say?" I had to know.

Serge grinned. "I apologized and told him that Fitzy was aiming for the Pakistani."

Fitzy's color was returning to a more normal pasty-white. I rammed a hand in the small of his back and sent him stumbling back toward the Marhaba Complex. As we crossed Qatar Street, I heard the unmistakable, cascading screech of a hundred loudspeakers as prayer call broke across the city. Looking at my watch, I saw it was 4 A.M. A new day was about to dawn.

CHAPTER
TWELVE

"Who gives a hairy shit, Duffman? Fucking Kirby Benson can go to fuckin' hell as far as I'm concerned. Son of a bitch has done a runner!" Frank was his usual incoherent self. He had rolled in over the weekend, and amazingly enough, found his way into the office.

"What's a runner?"

"A runner," Perry offered, "refers to an act committed by a disgruntled employee. The employee in question leaves the country, and therefore the contract, without any notice or warning. In other words, he runs."

I shook my head. "I don't think so, Frank. He didn't take anything with him. All his clothes, his books, his typewriter, everything's still in his room. I mean, even his dirty underwear."

"So? Son of a bitch probably forgot to take them."

Something was wrong with Frank's sequence of events. I mean, the man was standing there with half his shirttail tucked in and half out. The slacks looked like they had been washed in the Nile, and his tie, which oddly enough was knotted correctly, was stained with yesterday's breakfast. He heaved his briefcase up on the desk and opened it. Empty. "Where's the fucking checkbook, Fitzy? How the fuck can I do payroll without the fucking checkbook?"

"Uh, Frank," Fitzy said. "Payday's not until next week."

Frank sat down heavily. "Well, hell, I'll go ahead and pay this week. Boys have been doing a pretty good job." He nodded, for punctuation I suppose, then lay his head on his desk.

"Jesus, Fitzy! Why the hell did you let him come to work?" Perry's voice was close to shattering glass. I'd never seen Perry so mad.

"He insisted. And I'm hung over."

"You're both lucky that drunken Russian fool didn't hit a Kuwaiti. You'd be paying blood money out the wazoo."

"Huh?"

"If a Kuwaiti gets killed in a traffic accident, the family will demand blood money, usually a sum they figure that person would have made over the course of his life. It's not pleasant. But forget that. If Nasser sees Frank, we're all in deep shit. Especially with this cheating thing going on."

"What cheating thing?" Frank asked, rousing himself to look at Perry with one eye.

"We'll tell you later." I personally thought that was awfully kind. I mean, after all, it was Frank who instigated the cheating.

"Naw, tell me now."

"Here, Frank," Perry said softly. "Take two of these and call us in the morning." He shoved two pills in Frank's hand and gave him a glass of water. Frank obediently tossed them down and chased them with coffee.

"What was that?" I asked.

"Rohypnol," Perry answered.

"What's Rohypnol?"

"They call it the 'date-rape drug', or 'roofies'," Perry advised me. "Slip it in their drink and they never know what hit them." He checked his watch. "In about ten minutes, we'll have Fitzy and a couple of the boys carry him out to the car."

"Kuwaiti alert!" George wiggled into the room, his mustache moving a mile a minute. "The colonel and Major Nasser headed this way."

I stepped into the hallway. Sure enough, the two officers were striding down the hall. Somebody must have told them that Frank was finally in the office. So much for operational security. Looking in the other direction, I saw the young Jufain and another soldier smoking cigarettes just outside the main door.

"Jufain! *Yella!*"

"What, teacher?"

"Hurry! *Yella!*" I pointed inside the office, and then retreated in there just as Nasser and the colonel hit the halfway line down the hall.

"Get out of the way!" I yelled at George.

Perry poked his head out. "What?"

"Poor Frank's had a relapse, right?" I was a model of intonation, turning the statement into a question with just the right change in pitch on the last word.

"Right," Perry agreed.

"Damn right," Fitzy concurred.

"Ughh!" Frank stammered, trying to raise his head from the desk. But the Rohypnol had obviously put Frank under in record time.

"Jufain! In here! *Yella!*" I pointed to Frank, now face down on the desk. "Please! Help him! *Yella!*" I was quickly exhausting my nonexistent Arabic.

Perry came to the rescue with a couple of pointed sentences. By the time Nasser and his boss stepped on George on the way in, Jufain and companion had Frank up in their arms and were bearing him away.

"Wait a minute!" No mistaking the sound of authority; Nasser's command voice echoed off the windows. He slammed a hand in Jufain's chest, stopping the entourage cold.

"No time," I countered, moving forward to clear a path for our stretcher bearers. "Frank's had a relapse. Come back later when we can talk."

"Is he drunk?" Nasser asked, sniffing.

"He's sick." That much, at least, was true. Frank *was* sick. But then I suppose there are subtle differences between alcoholism, drug addiction, and strep throat. "Relapse."

Nasser looked at me with those cold eyes of his. "Don't jerk me around, Duffy." What he didn't say was, "I have your balls in my hand and I'm about to squeeze." But I got the message.

Jufain got his burden out of the room.

Nasser looked at his superior carefully. "We need someone to argue our case at the embassy. Brigadier General Quentin Murphy with the Office of Military Cooperation–Kuwait has demanded a meeting to answer charges of cheating against the Kuwait Air Defense Brigade."

"To 'answer charges,' Nasser? Sounds a little stiff. Don't you really mean talk the matter over with them?"

"Yeah, okay. I was being a little dramatic. But, boys, this thing has gotten out of control." Nasser stopped and lit a cigarette. "Now, we all know what happened. We've just got to make sure that we know 'exactly' what happened."

Time to get the old stories straight. Can't have the customer saying one thing and the subcontractor another. "What exactly *is* the story? I mean, since I wasn't here for the event in question." I gave them a perfect opportunity to make up their own story.

"Simple," Fitzy began. "They're excellent students and mastered the material without any hitches."

We all turned and looked at him.

"Two of the students were exceptional. They worked out a complicated method of communicating with the others in the laboratory. The examinees were able to transmit the questions to the two geniuses and they provided the answers. The investigation is ongoing, but the U.S. government should be aware that the responsible parties will not go unpunished." Perry actually got all that out in one breath.

"And," I kicked in, "since no answer keys were stolen, this is an internal Kuwaiti matter and will be dealt with accordingly."

Nasser nodded. "Not bad," Nasser said. "It should work. Now, which one of you is going to come to the meeting?"

Fitzy headed out the door at a trot. "I have to go down to the book room and count books."

Perry smiled broadly. "I have other work to do."

Nasser grabbed me by the arm. "Duffy, you're becoming my favorite American. The meeting is Monday at 10 A.M. We'll meet here and drive over together. Make sure you're dressed appropriately."

I looked down at my wrinkled shirt and tie. "Are you saying I don't dress appropriately?"

"I'm saying your maid's either on vacation or you don't have a maid. Don't worry, Duffy," Nasser continued. "I'll let you drive my BMW."

"So," I explained to Karen that night on the phone. "I'll be at the embassy on Monday. Gee, maybe I'll get to see you before they march me out to the firing squad."

"Oh, Duffy. Is anything ever easy for you?" The wistfulness in her tone sounded strangely like pity. And just as soon as they start pitying you, they dump you. I'd seen it happen before, usually to me. "Listen. After you finish your meeting, go to Marine Post One and put in a call to me. We'll eat lunch in the cafeteria."

"Marine Post One. Is that where they take you to be shot?"

"Of course, but they always give you a last request." Her voice lowered conspiratorially. "Tell them you have to eat lunch with me, and then I'll smuggle you out the back way."

"What a woman! What did I do to deserve you?"

"Nothing yet. But come over tonight and I'll give you a chance to earn my devotion."

"Ummhh, yeah, well, I, have to do something for a friend."

"Duffy? You're not still trying to chase Serge's daughter, are you?" That warm, voluptuous voice shifted to one of maternal warning. "All you're doing is getting yourself in trouble."

"Hey. Trouble seems to follow me. I mean Kirby's missing. I've got to go to an inquisition conducted by some American general. And my Russian diplomat neighbor wants me to follow his daughter."

"How long's Kirby been missing?" She swiftly avoided the brewing conflict.

"Not long enough. Must be about three days now."

"I think you should report it."

"To who? I told Frank, but he's convinced that Kirby just took a hike."

"Yeah, but since when did you put any credence in anything Frank says? You could report it to the U.S. consul."

"What will he do?"

"I'm not really sure. Notify the Regional Security Office. They'll notify the local authorities. Somebody in the consulate will start the process of notifying the next of kin."

"A lot of notification going on, but I don't see a lot happening to find Kirby."

"We both know that that's up to the locals. They're going to go about it in their own way."

"Which could take forever," I pointed out.

"Which could take forever," she agreed. "Okay, well, try to stay out of trouble. I'll see you tomorrow night."

"*Inshallah.*" At least I didn't say "*boukara* and *maalesh.*"

I hung up and wandered down the hall toward Kirby's room. A faint hint of cigarette smoke and stale body odor still lingered around the door. Sort of reminded me of my father. Daddy had his own personal scent that was also crafted from cigarette smoke and sweat. I remembered then that Kirby had a son, a teenager. It occurred to me that Kirby might have an address or something.

Carefully, slowly, I opened the door. Can't really say what I was afraid of. Maybe that the ever-promiscuous Debbie would leap out and pounce on me. Or the Bangladeshi in the orange coveralls would slip out from under the bed and assault me. How life had changed. Just a few months ago, I was worried about creditors leaping out of closets.

Kirby's room was just as I'd last seen it. Overflowing ashtrays on the nightstand, dirty underwear on the floor. I scanned the desk, not sure if it was safe to touch anything. People who stole typewriter ribbons might booby-trap the place, too. Hell, Kirby could have booby-trapped the whole place. Finally, peeking out from beneath a stained tee shirt on the floor, an address book showed. Slipping it out with two fingers, I saw a slight blue ribbon marking a page.

"Calvin Benson," it read. "1818 N. Broad, San Francisco." There was a telephone number. Had to be his son. I copied the information down. On the edge of the desk, hidden behind a stack of books, was a photograph. A kid. It was an old photo; Kirby had made it clear his son was in college. Poor kid. Maybe twelve. In a blue and white football uniform. Cute. Even if he did have Kirby's nose. I sat down on the edge of the bed and stared at the photograph. How did a kid this normal-looking end up with a father like Kirby Benson?

Benson, Benson, Benson, I thought. You poor old fart. Either he kept his notes or manuscript on his big story hidden and took the ribbon out of the old typewriter, or somebody else had done the honors. In my mind, that somebody else was looking better and better as the culprit. I looked at the kid again and wondered if he'd picked up any of his father's traits. Hopefully just the good ones. I thought about that for a second and couldn't remember any good ones.

I considered having the maids come in the next day and clean up, but somehow, I couldn't face the idea of Kirby coming back and finding it clean. In the face of that, I shut the door and tried to forget that I lived next door to Three Mile Island.

I wandered back into the living room, after helping myself to some of Kirby's wine. What could have happened to him? Or, to look at it another way, what the hell was he up to? Could he have gone undercover to try to break this big story of his? Kirby was capable of anything. He had the brain of a porcupine and the tenacity of a snapping turtle. For all I knew, he was even then dressed in a *dishdasha*, sneaking around Dasman

Palace, trying to get a look at the emir's secret files on chemical weapons.

The question at the heart of it all was simple: was Kirby really onto something, or were the fundamentalists, like this Abdulmohsen character, using him for their own purposes? Just in the short time I'd been in Kuwait, it had become obvious that the antigovernment boys were always looking for a new way to slam the establishment. And that's pretty tough in a country where the government controls just about every avenue of approach. Why not use a crazy American?

Of course, that didn't answer the question of Kirby's whereabouts. Unless the little idiot had gone undercover. I shook my head. Part of me said that if anything was to be done about Kirby, I was going to have to do it. Frank couldn't have cared less. Perry seemed to have no opinion on the matter. Fitzy was, well, Fitzy, and that meant he would just as soon throw Kirby out the window. Unfortunately, I had my hands full with other, more pressing matters. Like perjuring myself in front of an American general. Or giving false testimony. Not to mention the never-ending saga of Serge's daughter.

Yeah, I decided as I went to the fridge for more wine, Kirby could go hang. Too many other fish to fry. Besides, he was a reasonably mature adult. He could take care of himself.

—◆—

"Hey, man! What's up?"

I had to learn to start locking my door.

Fitzy assaulted my living room at full speed. "Got anything to read? Man, I'm fucking bored and out of good reading material!"

"What do you consider good reading material?" This ought to be worth a chuckle.

Fitzy shook his head with a sort of "it-doesn't-matter" kind of shrug. "I'll take anything. I just finished Milton's *Paradise Lost* for like the third time."

"You read Milton?"

That infectious grin spread across his face. "Of course. Supposed to read all the great books, right? I've read Milton, Dante, Melville, Shakespeare—"

"Which play?"

He looked at me with raised eyebrows, like I'd offended him. "All of them. And the sonnets too. 'Venus and Adonis', 'The Rape of Lucrece', all that stuff."

"Fitzy, just the other day at work, you asked me to help you write a letter home. But, if I'm supposed to believe you, you've read half the Boston Public Library."

"I mean, I just like to read. I don't spend a lot of time writing or nothing like that."

"What else do you read? I mean besides literature."

"I like history. That's what my degree's in." He scratched his curly red hair. "A little psychology, some philosophy."

"You continually amaze me, Fitzy. Just when I think I've got you pegged, you come out with some new revelation."

"Thanks, Duffy." He beamed.

I turned around and headed to my bedroom. "I think I've got a copy of Emerson's essays back here somewhere."

"Oh." The disappointment rang across the room. "I was hoping you brought some new fuckbooks, you know, *Gallery* or *Playboy* or something. But I'll take Emerson if that's the best you have."

Yeah, Fitzy never ceased to amaze me.

"Hey, Duff? Any news about Benson? Frank was asking about him."

"Nothing I know of, but then, I haven't been out looking for him, either."

"Yeah, I know, but Frank's afraid of what Providence might say if we can't find him. You know, doesn't look good to lose a teacher."

"I didn't figure Frank was afraid of anything," I continued, still headed toward the bedroom.

"Every once in a while, when he's sober. Say, what are you doing tonight? Wanna scarf some pizza?"

"Naw, I've got to see a friend."

"Not that embassy chick?"

I stopped halfway to the bedroom and turned around. "How did you know I was still seeing her?" I'd made it a point to keep my mouth shut about Karen around the guys.

Fitzy grinned. "You can't keep anything quiet in this country, Duff. Serge told me. Says she's a real hot babe, but she'll probably dump you. Says that she's got a reputation in the diplomatic community for scoring on guys and then trashing them. Like she's collecting trophies."

"Thanks for the warning." With anybody else, I'd probably have been royally pissed off. But, with Fitzy, it just didn't seem appropriate. "But no, that's not what I'm planning to do." In other words, Fitzy, I'm not telling you.

By the time I shut the door behind him, the phone was ringing and I forgot about the advice. It was Serge, of course. Marina was off on one of her nightly voyages. So, therefore, was I.

Just like before, she waited behind the apartment complex for a taxi. Different company this time, I noticed, Al-Bahar Taxi. Smart, if she didn't want cabbies to get too suspicious, and cabbies were notoriously suspicious in Kuwait, especially with females. More than once I'd heard about some Western female taking a cab home after a party and the cabbie delivering her to the closest police station instead. In the Muslim world, a drunk female is a criminal.

This time, I figured I knew where she was going, and to test my theory, I simply drove ahead of them, avoided the Bint Al-Deek restaurant, and parked in a mosque parking lot a little further away from the aerobics studio, where I didn't have to worry about the Egyptian curb service. The only thing that bothered me was that the mosque was Shia'a. I could tell by the architecture, particularly the green dome. Only the Shi'ites, considered the most radical sect of all Muslims, painted their mosques green. But I was between prayer calls, so I figured I was fairly safe.

The taxi pulled up, discharged Marina, and sped away. Within minutes, she was joined by another girl. I watched intently now; this was the part I'd missed on the last trip. Hardly five minutes passed before a black Mercedes pulled up; the girls hopped in, and off they went.

The driver of the Mercedes wasted no time pulling a U-turn at the Tunis Street exit. Taking a deep breath, I zipped in between a couple of Nissan trucks and finally caught up with the Mercedes around the Highway 50 exit. And that was a good thing, because Highway 50 is where it turned off.

I floated back two cars behind them, driving normally, not craning my neck. And the Mercedes behaved rationally, or as rationally as Kuwaiti traffic permitted.

Finally, the car got close to the Holiday Inn Crowne Plaza in Farwaniya. The hotel, with its golden, gleaming windows, sticks out like a sore thumb in the middle of the brown-stoned buildings of Kuwait. Kuwait doesn't have wooden houses, not really, and damned few red brick homes. The lower classes live in adobe-style buildings, some high-rise type, some single-story affairs. But the middle class and up go for the gusto—stone, usually white or off-white, covered most exteriors, and that made for real confusion when driving around. One landmark looked just like another. Except for buildings like the Holiday Inn. So, I breathed a sigh of relief when it looked like they were turning into the parking lot. At least I could explain to Serge where they went. I figured, okay, what the hell; they're either checking in or just going for coffee, Marina, her pal, and whoever was driving the big black Mercedes.

Unfortunately, they weren't going to the Holiday Inn. That old black Mercedes sped right past and headed deep into Farwaniya, an area I knew virtually nothing about. The streets are narrow, usually half-covered with sand. Most of the buildings are low-rent apartments, leased mainly to Egyptian laborers and some Indians and Pakistanis. I think George, our clerk, had an uncle who lived in the area.

The other car couldn't move too fast in the narrow lanes, so I didn't have much trouble keeping up. With my window rolled down, I could smell pungent curry and garlic, minced lamb on the grill, and the moldy, stale odor of crumbling mudbricks. It was an odd melange of scents, but one I was beginning to enjoy.

After a few minutes of curving in and out of side streets, the Mercedes stopped in front of a dilapidated villa, three stories with a surrounding wall. The girls slipped in the gate and the Mercedes cruised on down the street and out of sight.

I parked a block away in front of a more upscale complex, ensuring first that I had a good, straight shot at the villa. For some reason, I'd supposed that Marina's adventure would be more cut and dried. You know, like a sign out front saying "Marina's boyfriend lives here." But no. They had gone into an anonymous villa in a land of anonymous villas. And I got to sit out front on stakeout with absolutely zero reading material.

But for the next half hour, I was fascinated. Just like the Mercedes, a parade of cars pulled up, discharged their passengers, and disappeared. Must have been about fifteen over the next thirty to forty-five minutes. After the first two or three, the passengers were exclusively male, all different shapes, sizes, and nationalities, mostly Western with a handful of Asians.

I'd heard about some of the parties in Kuwait. Usually they held them down at the chalets on the coast, out of the watchful eye of the authorities. Fitzy told me about one party he went to: Bedouin women, completely covered—veils and everything. Two steps in the door and the veils and everything else came off. They were naked as jaybirds underneath.

Maybe that was what this is, I thought. Not every father's ideas of where his daughter should spend her evenings, but if she wasn't into anything worse than the local party scene, then it wasn't that bad.

One thing bothered me. No *haris*. Every villa of any size always had some Third Worlder as a live-in caretaker or *haris*. They were always puttering around outside, especially at night, generally making a nuisance out of themselves. But not here.

Flashing the ceiling light long enough to check my watch, I saw it was just after midnight. The traffic into the villa had died down, just an occasional car dumping an occasional passenger. I'd give it another thirty minutes and then hang it up for the night. At least I could tell Serge *where* his daughter was going, even if I couldn't tell him *what* she was doing.

To pass the time, I started counting burned-out street lights. The yawns set in after a couple of minutes of that, and I started arguing with myself over the timetable. Was another twenty minutes or so really going to make that much of a difference? What were the odds that Marina was going to come out before 12:30 or so? So, true to my nature, I started to turn the key, just as another vehicle stopped about a half block away from the villa. But something about this one was different, and I shut off the engine.

It was a red Jeep Cherokee with black trim, unlike the Mercedes and BMWs that had come and gone over the last hour or so. Just normal, Kuwaiti license tags. Two men got out, one from each side, and they circled the Jeep to converge on the rear end. Both men were tall; both were Western. One wore a shirt and tie, the other a dark, collared pullover and chinos.

They kept glancing around, trying not to be obvious about it. One stood watch while the other slipped a key into the back hatch and turned. Even down the street, I could hear the click.

As the hatch slid up, both men reached inside and yanked an object, like a giant sack of potatoes, out. It rolled onto the ground with a thud, and the man in the pullover grabbed it and jerked it up. The sack of potatoes was a man.

Not only that, I realized, as my fists tightened on the wheel, but that sack of potatoes was Kirby Benson.

CHAPTER
THIRTEEN

Wherever Kirby had been for the last three days, I never wanted to go there. His eyes were puffed and red like overripe tomatoes. In the dim brightness of the tail lights, I could make out abrasions on both cheeks. He could stand, but just barely, his legs shuddering underneath him worse than Frank's.

With one guy acting as lookout, the other shoved Kirby down the street toward the villa. Kirby stumbled about three steps and fell flat on his face. Both guys picked up his sorry bag of bones and hustled him to the gate and then inside.

I sat in the Galant with my jaw bouncing like a basketball on the steering wheel. Whatever the old fraud had done, whoever he had pissed off, he didn't deserve such a beating. "God in heaven!" my dearly departed mother would say. At that point it looked like Kirby was going to see Mom before I did.

Glancing in my rearview, I noticed a Kuwaiti police car turn the corner and head in my direction. I knew I should stay, but

I didn't need the police taking an unhealthy interest in me. What excuse could I give? Officer, I followed the Russian consul's daughter here and then I saw one of my buddies being hustled in by a couple of heavies. Yeah, right. In a pig's eye. Or make that, in a sheep's eye. Wouldn't want to be accused of being culturally insensitive.

"Sorry, Kirby," I muttered, tripping the ignition and shifting into gear. "Better luck next time." And with that, I was out of there.

<hr />

"Now, Duffy. You didn't realize the importance of this story," Kirby told me as he dangled at the end of a rope. One eye fell out of its socket and drooped over a cheek. Blood seeped from his ears, running darkly onto a white shirt. "I told you it was important."

"Yeah, Kirby. You told me. But how was I supposed to know you were telling the truth. Normally, you're full of shit." I floated somewhere below him, not really standing on anything, but not falling either.

"You haven't known me long enough to know whether I'm full of shit or not. Besides, you didn't even try to come in and get me."

"C'mon, Kirby. Would you have busted in to get me?"

"No," he conceded with a bloody frown. "But you're not as important as I am. Anyway," he continued as the other eye fell with a wet splat, "it really doesn't matter now. I'm dead, you see, and now my son will never know that his father discovered the story of the century. And it's all your fault."

I hung my head, my face running hot with shame. And then I began falling.

I woke up.

The sweat ran down both temples and my legs were shaking so hard I couldn't stop them, even when I bolted upright and reached down and grabbed my ankles.

Looking over at the nightstand, I saw the glow of the clock hands—3:30 A.M. I'd only been in bed two hours. Of all the nightmares to have—Kirby Benson hanging from the ceiling. To walk in and see it in real life was one thing, but to dream it was a bit much. Besides, I told myself, the last time I saw Kirby, he was still alive. Not moving very well, mind you, but definitely alive.

An hour later, I kept mumbling to myself through the coffee-making process. Switching on CNN, I prayed for some international crisis powerful enough to divert Brigadier General Quentin Murphy from Kuwait to, say, Alaska. Maybe Russia would invade across the Bering Strait. But nothing of any consequence was happening, at least, that is, nothing that would affect Kuwait for the next forty-eight hours or so. Hell, Saddam Hussein wasn't even starting anything, and he oozed aggression and hostility.

Two hours later, after watching Bernard Shaw explain for the third time how El Niño stood to affect the entire world, I knotted my tie and headed to the parking lot.

"Duffy! How you been, man? What the hell's happening?" One of the other teachers, a glad-hander whose name I couldn't remember, was jumping up and down beside the Galant. All I could remember about him was that he always had something going, something that was going to make him rich. "I got a great gimmick for you, man! Absolutely great! We'll make tons of money! Quit teaching all this garbage and live the good life!"

"Yeah, like what?" At that point, I was open to anything.

"A cookbook!" He said it like he invented the idea.

"A cookbook. That's going to make us rich?" Somehow the logic eluded me.

"Not just any cookbook. A diplomatic cookbook!"

"What, are we going to write the recipes in code?"

The guy's face wrinkled in disappointment. "You're not getting the picture."

"Paint it a little clearer."

He leaned up against the car. "See, we solicit recipes from all the embassies all over the world. Then, we put it together into the U.S. State Department's official cookbook."

"Won't the State Department have something to say about that?"

He grinned. "That's where you come in." He draped his arm around me. "You get your girlfriend to call up one of her buddies in the State Department and get their authorization. Once that's done, we'll make a mint."

I slung my arm around his shoulder. "I'm tired, frustrated, and irritable. Go jack somebody else off before I create a recipe for minced English instructor." Damn! Fitzy and his big mouth. Did everybody on the contract know about Karen? The guy stomped away, grumbling about ingrates, and I still couldn't remember his name.

Fitzy bopped out of his building and sauntered across the lot. "Morning. It's a great morning, you know? The kind of morning that makes you glad to be alive, even if it's in Kuwait."

Granted, the sky was blue. But it was about 120 degrees on the pavement, with not even a hint of relief in the breeze. But after the last few days, the weather was the last thing that bothered me.

"Fitzy, did you find it necessary to tell everybody in Kuwait that I have a girlfriend?"

"Naw. I just told Perry, and he must have told Jack. You worry too much."

"Why would Perry care?" For some reason that bothered me. Fitzy shrugged. "I think he wanted to know if you were taken."

That's all I needed. I leaned against the car. "Frank staying in today?" I ventured after a few seconds.

144

"Yeah. He still hasn't gotten over that Rohypnol. I stopped up to see him last night and all he could say was something about 'did Perry take advantage of me again?' I didn't want to ask any questions so I just left."

"Fitzy," I began. "What if I told you that I thought Benson was in some sort of trouble?"

"What kind of trouble?"

"Bad trouble. Bad enough to get him killed, maybe."

Fitzy grinned. "Leave him alone. He deserves whatever he gets. What makes you think he's in trouble?"

"Nothing. Just a thought." If I told Fitzy, he'd probably drive over to Farwaniya and help the boys out. Poor Kirby wouldn't stand a chance. Maybe in another life Fitzy had been part of the Spanish Inquisition.

Whistling, Fitzy climbed into his Swiftie and blasted off.

I crawled into the Galant, strapped myself in, and started for the base. Fitzy was one of those people you couldn't get mad at. As Serge would say, "*Walla*, I swear it."

Well, Kirby aside, at least I had something to tell Serge about Marina. Maybe that would get him off my tail. Benson would just have to wait. I put my brain through a series of mental acrobatics, trying to figure out the Kirby Benson caper, but nothing really came together. The only thing I knew for certain was that it added up to trouble. And by that time, I was breezing past the guards and onto the base.

I tried to remember what day of the week it was—Tuesday, no, Sunday, that's right, Sunday. I kept forgetting that Sunday in Arabia is like Tuesday, or something like that. Not even the calendar, it seemed, worked like what I was used to.

I pulled into the parking lot beside Fitzy's Swift. He had waited patiently for me to catch up, and then we headed to the building, greeting our hand-holding, cheek-pecking students as we walked. Jufain jumped out of a group of them with something in his hand. Visions of John Hinckley flashed across my brain. Oh, Jesus! Here it comes! But, no, Jufain held out a bouquet of flowers with a big-toothed grin. "For you, teacher. For you."

I stood there a second, uncomprehendingly watching this Bedouin kid offering me a present. Then Fitzy whispered in my ear: "Take them, idiot. It's an insult if you don't."

I accepted the gift and tried to smile, but flowers from another guy is new to me. But I made the best of it, and followed Fitzy into the office.

"What was that all about?" he asked, stashing his briefcase on the conference table and whipping the newspaper open to the crossword.

"I have no idea." Checking to make sure nobody could see, I stashed the flowers in the trashcan.

"You shouldn't do that," Perry's soft, mellow voice called from the doorway. "He was just showing his appreciation and affection. Besides, they're beautiful."

"Then you keep the flowers," I suggested, a little more curtly than I intended.

Perry turned away, moisture at the corner of his eyes.

"Sorry, Perry. Just under a lot of pressure these days."

"I'm sure," he answered a little haughtily and trounced out.

"Don't worry about Perry, man," Fitzy counseled without looking up from the crossword. "PMS. You're too sensitive, Duffy. Relax. Chill out." For the first time since I'd known him, Fitzy actually showed irritation at something other than Kirby Benson. So, I left him alone.

"Boss?" George stood in the doorway with a frightened look on his face. "Trouble with Mr. Jack. Better come."

As I came within sight of Jack's classroom, I saw an armload of students milling around. I checked my watch. Two minutes to break. Hitting the door with a vengeance, I found Jack sitting in a chair up against the wall, red-faced, puffing, and holding his arm.

"Jack, are you okay?" The man's having a heart attack and I ask him if he's okay.

He looked up at me with sad eyes and let go of his arm long enough to rub his bald pate. "I think so. I'm so sorry, Duffy. I just don't know what happened. One minute I was fine, and then the next, well, it was like everything turned brown." He paused long enough to take a deep breath. "Then, the next thing I knew, a couple of the boys had put me in this chair." He tapped the chair with both hands, as if to make sure it was real.

"Jack, I think we should send you over to the hospital. Have you looked over."

"That's very sweet of you, Duffy, but I'll be all right if you just let me sit here for another minute or two. We're right in the middle of something important, the future perfect."

I stepped back for a second and looked at Jack, something I hadn't really done since the first day. Mostly what I knew about him came from other people; he was an old Middle Eastern hand with about thirty years of experience. But I wondered why he was out here at his age. Just measuring the wrinkles, I figured he must be about sixty-five or so. I'm pretty sure I don't want to be in Kuwait teaching English when I'm sixty-five.

"C'mon, Jack. Give it a rest. You've done your job for the day. I'll cover it or get McBride to catch it." Tucker McBride, a burly oaf, was currently exiled to the laboratory.

Jack's eyes shot at me like a laser and his blood pressure must have hit stroke level. "You will not! I'll not have my boys subjected to that idiot's ranting and raving!"

"Obviously, you're not as sick as I thought you were," I answered him. "How long have you been teaching out here, anyway?" I grabbed a chair. The break had started.

"Oh, about thirty-five years."

"Yeah?"

"Yes. I started out in Afghanistan, working as a bookkeeper for a construction company. My first teaching job was in Saigon back in 1963 and 1964." Jack leaned his head back against the wall and closed his eyes.

"How was that?"

"Good. Saigon was beautiful back in those days. Then came seventeen years in Tehran. Now, Duffy, that was marvelous."

"Seventeen years?"

"Yeah," he said, his voice growing soft. "I ran the English program for Bell Helicopter with the Iranian Air Force. Tehran—all of Iran—was so beautiful. You have those wonderful mountains up by the Caspian Sea and then the desert to the south with the Bedouins. I could have lived there forever. Got married in Iran."

"You were married? I thought you were—"

His eyes flew open, laughing at me gently. "I am. She had a lover in the states—an Iranian doctor completing his residency. Since he was an alien, he couldn't sponsor her, and she couldn't get a green card without marrying an American. Her family had become like my own, and I agreed to marry her so she could be with the doctor. Soon after, she got her green card and left for the states. I divorced her so she could marry him." Jack was talking too much.

"And everybody lived happily ever after." I couldn't help myself.

"Not quite. The doctor had already found himself an American wife by the time she got there. I'm not sure what ever happened to her."

His color was still not back to normal, and he kept rubbing his arm.

"Jack, I'm going to get Fitzy to take you down to the hospital, just to be on the safe side." I raised a hand to stop his protest. "I'll cover your class. I won't let McBride anywhere near them."

"Thank you, Duffy. I think it was just an anxiety attack or something, but maybe you're right. I'm certainly not as young as I used to be."

Maybe it was going to be an okay day: a bouquet of flowers and an averted heart attack. I rubbed my hands together in anticipation. This ought to be a blast, I thought, as George fetched Fitzy to take Jack to the military hospital, and I steeled myself for my first experience in a Kuwaiti classroom.

I took a deep breath and plunged in.

"Good afternoon!" I said firmly and loudly.

"Good afternoon!" repeated twelve smiling Kuwaiti airmen.

Well, this was a promising start. I relaxed a little. What was it Jack said he was teaching—the future perfect? That shouldn't be too bad, I told myself.

"I will have gone." That sounded good. "Repeat after me." All eyes focused on Mr. Duffy. "I will have gone."

"Ahh weel have goan," came twelve Kuwaiti-Tennessee accents.

Oh, my God! "No, you can't say it like that."

"Naoow, ya'll cain't say hit lack thet."

I was in the Twilight Zone. It sounded like I was opening a Kuwaiti chapter of the KKK. "Oh, shit!" I stammered.

"Awhh, shee-it," repeated my totally obedient class, all smiling proudly.

I threw up my hands. Not only was I ill-suited to save Kuwait from Saddam Hussein, Marina Malenkova from slutdom, and Kirby Benson from himself—I couldn't teach English, either.

In desperation, I snatched up a textbook and flipped through it frantically. Great! A written exercise guaranteed to keep them busy through the rest of class. As enthusiastic as they were, it should be a piece of cake.

I flipped the book around and pointed to it. "Do—number—six," I explained slowly and carefully.

This they understood. And being trained, disciplined airmen, three of them immediately began working, eight put their heads down on the table and promptly went to sleep, and one opened a pad and started doodling.

I tapped a sergeant on the sleeve. "What's with them?" I pointed at the airmen.

He just shrugged. "They no like book work, Mr. Duffy."

I thought about trying to regain control, but then I realized I'd never been in control, and since half of them were already sawing some serious logs, I wandered over to my artist instead and glanced down at his sketch. He held it out proudly and I took it.

A swastika, and a pretty credible rendering of Adolf Hitler.

"Hitler?" I said.

The kid grinned from ear to ear. "Hitler number one, teacher."

"Why's that?"

"Because, teacher," he explained patiently. "Hitler kill Jews."

"Yeah," I said, stunned. I handed it back to him and went to help the trio that was actually trying to learn some English.

A couple of times, I was tempted to tell my neo-Nazi friend that Arabs weren't very high on Hitler's hit parade either. But, in the end, I didn't. Theoretically, I was there to teach English, not history.

—◡—

After class, I headed back up the hall, opting to drop in on the latrine to relieve a necessary call of nature. Unfortunately, the door was stuck.

I pushed.

It resisted.

I pushed harder.

It still resisted.

I put my shoulder into it like Refrigerator Perry, feeling the wood crack under my weight.

The door finally gave up the ghost, falling backward with a crash and a loud, mournful, humanlike groan.

Then I saw two pair of feet under the door and I realized that it *was* a human groan.

I reached down and grabbed the door, lifting it carefully off the couple beneath it.

"Perry! Good God!" Yes, it was Mohammed, the Bangladeshi teaboy, and Perry with his mouth firmly attached around Mohammed's dick. No wonder the door was jammed. "Did you ever hear of discretion?"

Mohammed, with a knot the size of a grapefruit swelling up on his head, looked at me with a mix of fear and pleading that exuded an odor all its own. I've heard that cats can smell fear. Right at that moment, I understood. They'd probably throw the poor guy *under* the jail. And Perry, all he'd get is thrown out of the country. Unless I did something quick.

I checked down the hall and saw a half-dozen guys headed in our direction. "Quick, Perry! Get him out of your mouth and stay down! Mohammed, *Yella*! Stand up! Zip up your pants."

Mohammed just sat there, staring at me wide-eyed, panting.

"Now, you idiot!" I reached down and yanked him to his feet.

For his part, Perry understood exactly what I was doing and lay there with his eyes closed, feigning a knock-out.

"Help me with the door!" I yelled, loud enough for everybody on the base to hear.

One of the sergeants was first on the scene. When he arrived, it looked for all the world like Perry had been trapped beneath the door and Mohammed and I were rescuing him. "What happened?" he asked, reaching in to help out.

"The door was stuck and Mohammed and I busted it open; we just didn't know Mr. Perry was on the other side."

He bought it hook, line, sinker, and pole.

Fitzy, who ran a close second, bought nothing. He checked out Mohammed's zipper and the knot on his forehead and grinned at me. "Poor Perry," Fitzy crooned. "Got caught in the—"

"—head by the door, exactly," I finished for him with a nasty look. "Help me get him on his feet."

So as more people gathered, Fitzy and I pulled Perry to his feet while Mohammed held the door up.

Perry extended himself to his full height and brushed off a few lingering pieces of splintered wood from his clothes. "Thank you, Duffy. Very kind of you."

"Gee, Perry," Fitzy said. He was pointing at Perry's mouth. "Damn, Perry! Caught you in the mouth, huh?"

I turned and noticed for the first time that Perry's lips were bloodied, but not noticeably damaged. Poor Mohammed. No wonder he was looking pained.

Perry fixed an icy gaze on Fitzy and smiled like a robot. "I'll survive. Thank you for your concern." Fitzy and I led him out and back down the hallway, leaving the Kuwaitis to handle the remaining carnage.

Once back in the office, Perry shook Fitzy's hand off. "Never, ever, expect any favors from me again. Duffy, here, was trying to salvage the situation, and you were ready to blab it all over the battalion."

"But—"

"And don't ask me again for that Syrian tart's phone number. You won't get it." With another icy stare tossed Fitzy's way, Perry stormed out of the office and out of the building.

"What Syrian tart?"

"Never mind." Fitzy was actually brusque. That was novel.

Actually, the more I thought about it, the better I liked Perry's option. Slapping the still-perturbed Fitzy on the back, I pointed him to the crossword. "Better finish up. I'm going back to the ranch."

—~—

Once back at the apartment, I fantasized about a languid afternoon spent drinking Kirby's wine and watching Hindi music videos, devouring a Dutch veal sirloin steak even then nestling in the refrigerator, but reality never matches the vision. I couldn't sit still. Obviously, I was experiencing too many stimuli, so I did what I always do back in the states when I can't sit still; I threw on my running shoes, grabbed my Walkman and Bob Seger's *Greatest Hits*, and headed down to Salmiya beach, just behind Kuwait's answer to Wal-Mart, the Sultan Center. After all, there was nothing that a good, hard sweat couldn't cure.

Few people wandered up and down the packed sand as I crawled out of the Galant and dodged traffic running across Gulf Street. Somebody, Perry maybe, had told me that the beach was a great place to pick up women. Perry's loss was my gain. The weather was a little more bearable; a thick, heavy bank of gray clouds had scudded across the desert, dragging some welcome, cooler breezes in its wake. Still hotter than hell, but not the kind of heat that you automatically think of in the middle of God's armpit. One day in the office I heard Fitzy say that if God was going to give the world an enema, he'd stick the hose in Kuwait and turn on the water. I had to admit he had a point. Not much here but sand, water, and some ugly buildings.

Anyway, I started down the beach at a reasonable pace. I tuned out everything, no Frank, no Perry, no Fitzy, no Serge. And despite the slight breeze, I broke a sweat quickly, setting markers and concentrating on reaching each one by one, not worrying about the next until its turn came. That was the only way I could make it through the long runs. Set a goal. Reach it. Set another. Reach it.

A watchhouse rose out of the beach like a finger, pointing at the sky. In one room, some five or six feet above ground level, I could see a Kuwaiti silhouetted against the sun, sipping his afternoon tea and gazing out into the Persian Gulf. On one level, I envied him the quiet and solitude, yet on another, my nature would never let me share in that kind of life. I looked too anxiously at planes flying overhead and ships driving through the water. So, I allowed him the unknown moment of jealousy and continued on down the beach, stopping finally at the base of a vanished monument sitting forlornly on the sand. I let the adrenaline wear down, savoring the flavor even as it disappeared.

After a few minutes, I wandered down to the edge of the beach, down where the sand disappeared beneath a ragged shoreline of huge, gray rocks jumbled together like a child's building blocks. Picking out a reasonably dry stone, I watched the big oil tankers, their bellies riding low, scudding out of the harbor and toward the open Gulf. Below me, in the shallows, schools of fish swirled and churned the waters. At that moment, I was pretty happy, pretty satisfied with where I was and what I was doing.

Until I saw the bleached-out hand, not six feet from me, floating among the rocks.

My heart thumped faster than after my run, and I stood to get a better look, balancing myself carefully on the uneven rock.

The body floated face down, one shoulder caught under the edge of a rock.

Looking back toward the watchhouse, I waved my arms and shouted, "*Yella! Yella!*"

The Kuwaiti looked out a side window and saw me shouting and jumping like a madman. Even from a distance I could see the frown growing on his face. He set his tea down and opened the window. "*Shinoo?*"

What the hell did *shinoo* mean? Oh, yeah, "what?" Since "there's a dead body floating in the water" was beyond my limited vocabulary, I continued jumping up and down and shouting at the top of my lungs. I began to attract a small crowd, and one man ventured close enough to see what I was pointing at.

I watched as his eyes grew wide and he turned to the watchhouse shouting in Arabic. The Kuwaiti yelled something that sounded like instructions and then turned back into his office.

The guy scrambled down the rocks, turning back after a second and looking at me strangely. "*Yella!*"

From his vantage point, I could see a little clearer. The body looked to be a male, stringy, sparse brown hair, but it was hard to tell anything about the man's build. The water bloated out the shirt so much that it looked like a big pink balloon. At least, I hoped that it was water puffing the shirt out. Years before, when I'd been a cop, I had helped pull a kid out of Stone's River. The boy had been in the water for about a week, and by the time the fish had finished with him, and the gases had engorged and distended his skin, there wasn't much recognizable.

We reached in and I grabbed one arm while the other guy maneuvered to free the shoulder. It took him a couple of minutes to unsnag the shirt from a jagged edge on the rock, and while he was doing that a larger crowd gathered. Women, completely veiled and covered, whispered to each other as the men shuffled around.

My stomach quit fluttering about that time, and I settled down to business. No skin slipped loose as my hand closed around the clammy wrist, so I knew he hadn't been down long. He was heavy, and as we struggled to pull him up on the rocks, I felt the muscles in my back begin to burn. Somewhere behind us, I heard the squeal of a police siren.

The sweat came back quickly as we dragged him on the rocks. As much as I wanted to quit reliving my days as a cop, it seemed like everything kept yanking me back. First, Serge and his daughter; now, a dead body floating in the water. Okay, I said to myself as we turned him over, there's nothing to get all wrapped up over.

Until I looked at the wide-eyed stare and the jagged edges of the little hole in the dead man's forehead. Then, I saw the gaping mouth and the crooked teeth inside. Bile burned my throat like acid.

Kirby Benson.

CHAPTER
FOURTEEN

After I finished heaving my guts into the Gulf, I stared out to sea. But I wasn't thinking about traveling; I was thinking about the night before when I watched Kirby shoved into the villa. Maybe if I'd done something then, the fat fart might still be alive. Then again, I might have ended up next to him.

Behind me, I could hear excited voices shouting in Arabic. The police got there while I was barfing and wisely left me alone. Of course, the fact that none of them spoke English probably didn't hurt any.

Suddenly, just as I got the vision again of that bullet hole in Kirby's head, somebody tapped on my shoulder. "Sir? Are you okay?"

It was a female voice, and I turned cautiously to see a forty-ish woman in slacks and a blouse standing over me. "Sir?" she repeated. "I'm with the U.S. Embassy. Were you the one who found the body?"

"Yeah."

"Can I ask you some questions?"

I looked at her as the fog began to lift. "Who are you?"

"I'm with the Regional Security Office at the embassy. The guy's an American. When something like this happens, I'm the one they call." Her voice was pleasant and comforting. She slipped a little notebook out and held a pencil over a blank page.

"Yeah, go ahead." I turned back to the Gulf.

"Your name?"

"Ed Duffy. Edward James Duffy."

"Where do you live, Mr. Duffy?"

"Here in Salmiya. In the Marhaba Complex."

"Who do you work for?"

"Arthur Watson, Inc. I teach with the Patriot Missile Program."

"Can you tell me what happened?"

"I was running on the beach. After I finished, I cooled down and walked over here to sit on the rocks. I just happened to glance over to the side and saw a hand sticking out of the water." The words came out mechanically, like twigs in my throat.

"And?" she prompted.

"And, I yelled out to the guy in the shack over there," I indicated the watchhouse. "Then, some other guy came over, saw the body, and told the Kuwaiti what was going on. We pulled the body out and I threw up." Somehow the admission caused me little embarrassment.

The woman smiled sympathetically. But I noticed a firmness in her eyes that belied her sympathy. She wouldn't have thrown up in a million years. This woman had seen some shit in her life; that much I could tell by looking.

"Well, thanks for the information. Somebody from the consular section will probably want to talk to you too." She turned to leave.

"Uh, ma'am?"

She turned around, stashing the notebook in her pants pocket.

"I know the guy."

"The dead man?" She paused and flipped back a page in her notebook. "Kirby Benson?"

"He was my roommate. He taught with the Patriot battalion, too."

"Home of record?"

"I'm not sure. He has a son living in San Francisco, but I don't think that's where he's from."

She lowered the notebook. "I take it you weren't real close?"

"It was difficult to be close to Kirby. He made it difficult."

"Do you have any idea why anybody would want to kill him?"

"You sound like a police officer," I noted.

Again, she smiled that soft little smile. "Well, let's just say that I'm the embassy's police officer. Besides, Mr. Duffy, confidentially, if we wait for the Kuwaitis to find out who killed Mr. Benson, you and I will be long gone. Anyway, the ambassador will want a full report, and it's my ass if I don't get it for him." She stopped and looked at me for a long second. "Haven't I seen you somewhere?"

"Maybe. I was at the embassy a couple of weeks ago for a party."

"That's right. You were the guy with Karen Solomon." Amazingly, though she had been polite, kind, and professional before, this new bit of information sent her into a complete attitude rotation. Now, we were buddies. "Listen, why don't you go wait in my Explorer? That way, I can keep the Kuwaitis off you for a while, at least until you catch your breath. Then we can finish up."

Grateful for the assist—whatever the reason—I climbed to my feet and headed to the dark green Ford truck she indicated. Alone in the cab, I couldn't hear the crash of the waves against the rocks anymore, and I realized then that I'd never enjoy the sound again.

After a couple of minutes, I looked up from the dashboard to see two men approaching the truck. Both wore ties; both wore windbreakers. One I'd never seen before, the other was all too familiar. And that was the one who knocked on the window with a smile.

Cracking open the door, I tried to smile in return. "Hello, Harvey." It was the inimitable Harvey Hanks, he of the "Don't Fuck With Us" business card. His sidekick was smaller, more immaculately groomed, with a permanent sneer. I knew instantly that I wouldn't like him.

"Ed Duffy!" Harvey squealed. "I'm right, right? Am I right?"

"Yeah, Harvey, you're right," I said wearily.

Harvey planted his hands on his hips and looked back to where the ambulance team had just loaded Kirby on a stretcher. "What a buttfuck, huh?"

I just nodded.

"Clarice says you knew the guy. That right?"

"Yeah, I knew him." I propped my head up on my knees and stared at the sand beneath the truck.

"Well?" The impatient voice belonged to Harvey's companion.

Looking up, I saw that "I'm-better-than-you" snarl in the man's face, and I wanted to smack him.

"Tell us what you know." He made condescension into an art form, sort of the way Josef Mengele made lampshades out of human skin.

"I'm afraid your pea-brain couldn't handle it." Duffy was on the offensive. Officious little shits like this guy turned me off.

"My name is L. Bruce Dalrymple, deputy chief of mission at the U.S. Embassy. I expect you to address me with the appropriate respect."

"Now, now, boys," Harvey jumped in. "No need for all this hostility. Bruce, why don't you go over and talk to Clarice. Duffy and I want to have a chat. Right, Duff? Am I right?"

"Sure, Harvey." I'd take Harvey and his used-car salesman pitch any day to an L. Bruce Dalrymple.

Dalrymple didn't like it. But he straightened his windbreaker and marched off across the beach. Harvey watched him go and then turned back as he leaned on the truck. "Don't pay any attention to Brucie, Duff. Didn't you ever read *The Ugly American?*"

"Saw the movie."

"Then you know Brucie's kind." He paused. "Listen, Duff. What's the deal with this Benson guy? Who would want to waste him?"

I decided right then that I liked Harvey. For all his oiliness, he was still an okay guy. So, I told him about Kirby and his big story, about all the weirdos in and out of the apartment. Abdulmohsen. The Bangladeshi. Debbie. My fears about this Abdulmohsen guy and his fundamentalist buddies and how they might be using Kirby for their own ends. Told him how Kirby disappeared. How Frank thought he'd taken a hike. How nobody else even missed the poor, sorry bastard. The only thing I didn't tell him was what I saw outside the villa in Farwaniya. That was one I kept to myself. How do you explain to somebody official that you were following the Russian consul's daughter, and by sheer chance saw your roommate hustled into the same bizarre villa?

161

For his part, Harvey stood there patiently and listened without interrupting until I finished. Then he just shook his head. "Boy, that's some shit sandwich, now ain't it, pardner?"

I nodded. "And then some."

"Well, now, I don't know, but you could be right about this Abdulmohsen character. He's a slick customer, and we've known for some time that he's mixed up in some shady business. His kind, Duff, they'd blow up a thousand Americans and smile about it. Shit, they wouldn't even miss a stroke if they were pounding their puds." He stopped for a second and smiled. "That's pretty much all of it, huh?"

"That's all I can remember. Jesus, Harvey! Don't tell me this stuff happens all the time. You seem so laid back."

Harvey shrugged. "Doesn't do any good to get too upset." He stopped and looked past me, out into the Gulf. "Hold your ears."

I followed his gaze and saw a Kuwaiti Coast Guard vessel moored about a half mile offshore. And just about the time I got my hands up to my ears, something exploded in a ball of fire and a geysering spout of water about five hundred yards off the ship's stern.

"Sea mine," Harvey explained. "Where was I? Oh, yeah, doesn't solve anything. But, no, we don't normally get too many Americans floating up on Salmiya beach with bullet holes in their foreheads. Can't seem to recall it happening before. That's probably why Brucie's panties are in a wad. He doesn't like surprises. And here he comes now." Hanks leaned over and patted me on the shoulder. "I'll handle him. You just sit still."

"Harvey, it's my turn," L. Bruce announced, his mouth turning up with irritation.

"Now, Bruce, just calm down. Duffy's had a rough day, and he's going to call it quits. But," Harvey held a hand up, catching Dalrymple in the chest, "he promises to come and see you tomorrow. Right, Duff?"

"Sure," I said, waving them both off. "Whatever you say." I had to go to the embassy the next day for the great Patriot inquisition. Why not sign up for two on the same day? They could only shoot you once.

L. Bruce wanted to say something. He opened his mouth and a half grunt started to spew out, but then he thought better and clamped it shut. "As long as you vouch for him, Harvey."

"You worry too much, Bruce. Doesn't he worry too much, Duffy? Am I right?"

"Absolutely, Harvey. Bruce worries far too much." I gave L. Bruce a look designed to stain his underwear, but he just smirked in response. He didn't spook easy; I'd give him that. "I'll be there."

"See that you are." And L. Bruce spun on his heels and headed back to the sidewalk.

"Get some rest, Duff. I'll try to be there tomorrow when you talk to Bruce. You've got my card, right?"

I nodded.

"If Abdulmohsen or any of those other characters show up, give me a call. Otherwise, steer clear of them. Don't try to track them down or anything. You got me? I don't want you getting into any trouble."

"Don't worry. The last thing I need is more trouble."

"That's my boy. Okay. I'll see you tomorrow. And, remember, if you need anything, call me."

"Right." And Harvey was gone.

A few minutes later, the embassy police officer appeared. I started to get up, but she waved me back down. "I'll give you a ride back to your place."

"What about the cops? Don't they want to talk to me?"

"No," she shook her head. "That other guy, the Iranian, told them all they wanted to know."

"But what about Kirby being my roommate and all?" Confusion was rearing its massive head.

She smiled. "We didn't tell them about that. By the time they figure it out, they'll have forgotten who found him. Nobody got your name, right? I mean nobody questioned you before we got there?"

"Right."

"There you go. Look, if we can avoid any further American involvement without really withholding evidence, then we do it. And the *mubahed*, the police investigators, are less than efficient. Nice guys, but no Sherlock Holmeses. Now, let's get you out of here."

One dead body. Two good Samaritans. And the Ugly American. Not bad for an afternoon's work.

CHAPTER
FIFTEEN

"Motherfucker! Son of a bitch is really dead?" Frank staggered across the room and blended a glass of wine with ethanol. He kicked the glass back and killed it.

Fitzy sat quietly on the couch. The only time in my admittedly short association with him that he had ever sat quietly anywhere. Perry stood, staring out the window.

"You know what?" Frank began, pouring himself another hemlock cocktail.

"What?"

Frank paused and held the glass up to the light. I wondered if he was checking the color, maybe to see if the blend was right?

"Son of a bitch probably died of AIDS."

"He had a bullet hole in his forehead, Frank."

Frank nodded sagely. "It's the complications that always get them."

Fitzy just kept staring at the floor. I'd never seen him like this before. Maybe it was guilt for the way he'd always hated Kirby. Sudden deaths spark a lot of emotions.

"Hey, Fitzy! What the hell's your matter?" Frank waved his freshly refilled glass toward the couch, losing about half of it in midflight.

"Leave me alone, Frank." Fitzy shook his head.

"Who pissed in your Wheaties, Fitz?" Frank wasn't about to let it die. He raised a drunken eyebrow at me. "Mama Fitzgerald's boy isn't happy tonight. Maybe he's missing his buddy Kirby too much."

But Fitzy wasn't even looking at Frank; he'd turned toward Perry. "Hey, were you serious about the Syrian chick?"

"Yes," Perry answered coldly. "Don't ask again."

"Isn't anybody here concerned about Kirby Benson?" I was at the end of the proverbial rope. One of our colleagues, one of our comrades-in-arms, was dead.

Frank turned and downed the rest of the wine. "Why? Son of a bitch is dead. Good riddance, I say. Jesus, Duffy, you get too sentimental over all this shit. Son of a bitch had to die sometime. Just our bad luck that he did it out here. Hell, I'll probably have to make a report back to Providence or something."

"It's lonely at the top, Frank," I consoled him.

"You bet your ass, Duffman. It's a bitch."

"Duffy, I want you to know that I appreciate your assistance earlier today. That was very kind of you." Perry refused to look at Fitzy.

"You're welcome, Perry. But, Jesus, couldn't you have picked a road less traveled?"

"I was caught up in the heat of the moment, you might say."

"I guess. Anyway, with all this other shit going on, that was one more thing we didn't need."

"All what shit?" Frank stopped in midgulp.

Fitzy, Perry, and I exchanged long looks. "Well," Fitzy began, "it's like this. The U.S. Army swears that the Kuwaitis got their hands on the ECL answer sheet and either fiddled with the scores or gave the answers to their boys. Major Nasser decided that Duffy should go with them to the embassy to smooth things over with the army boys."

Frank seemed to think hard about this situation. "Good," he said finally. "Glad to see you getting in the middle of things, Duffman. We'll make a senior instructor out of you yet. Fitzy, have I asked Providence to promote Duffman to senior instructor?"

Fitzy rolled his eyes. "Yeah, Frank, two or three weeks ago."

"Right. Just checking." He downed the rest of his wine. "Well, I'm gonna go barf now. You guys hit the road. Duffman, I think you should have a staff meeting tomorrow and lead the group in a memorial service for that faggot Benson."

"Frank!"

"No, no. It's only right. I mean he was your roommate after all."

Brigadier General Quentin Murphy was the picture of U.S. Army rigidity. I could tell just by looking at him that he conducted close order drill with his nose hairs. And any recalcitrant hair was immediately sent to the firing squad. His uniform was immaculate, his hair neatly and symmetrically colored in varying shades of gray.

Murphy sat at the end of a long conference table, flanked by a cadre of other U.S. Army officers, each in a contest to see who could sit the straightest. The conference room was at the top of the main stairs in the embassy, just past Marine Post One and through the incredibly heavy security doors guarding the embassy proper from the riffraff that made it past the main entrance.

I sat at the other end of the table, flanked by Major Nasser and his colonel. The general cleared his throat.

"We've convened this meeting to investigate the possibility that ECL answer sheets were compromised during the last administration. Major Bowles, would you read the comparison of scores between the next to the last administration and this last one?"

"Yessir. In both test administrations, approximately forty enlisted personnel from the Kuwait Air Defense Brigade were examined. During the earlier administration, only 10 percent of the examinees achieved an ECL of 50. At the most recent administration, 75 percent earned an ECL of 50 or above."

"We were very pleased," Major Nasser said with a smile. "Our men worked very hard."

Murphy harrumphed. "Yes, well, I'm sure that's true. But you must admit, Major, that a 650 percent increase from one test administration to the next is nothing short of remarkable."

"Under normal circumstances that would be true, General," I pointed out. "But these weren't normal circumstances. You see, we initiated a mandatory study hall period prior to the last ECL administration. I suspect that, to a large degree, that accounts for the dramatic increase in the results."

General Murphy looked at me without smiling. "Who are you?"

"I'm representing Arthur Watson, Inc. My name is Ed Duffy."

"Where's the project manager? I thought I gave instructions that he was to be here."

"He's suffering from strep throat, General."

"I see. Well, then, I guess you'll have to do." I felt like a bastard child. "So, your defense is that an extra hour a day of instruction has resulted in a 650 percent increase?"

"Partially." I glanced at Nasser and he nodded. "We have discovered that two of our more proficient students have developed a sophisticated method of communicating with the students taking the test. They were able to provide a significant number of answers. But no answer sheets were stolen, and, as protocol dictates in this situation, the Kuwaitis have begun their own investigation." In other words, G.I. Joe, back off.

"How many students were involved in this . . . ," the general paused, searching for the right word. "This . . . effort?"

"Preliminary indications are that only three or four students were actively engaged in communicating answers."

Murphy's eyes narrowed. "I'm assuming you're willing to provide a list of those personnel found to be culpable."

Nasser and I traded frowns. "That would be," I began, "inappropriate in the current situation. At least until the Kuwaitis finish their investigation."

"And I will, of course, receive a copy of any report generated by this investigation?" It really was a question.

The look I got from my coconspirators said basically, "You painted yourself into this corner; let's see you get out."

I shuffled papers for a minute. "Of course, General. You'll be provided with the report as long as it's not deemed critical to Kuwaiti national security."

"That's the biggest load of horseshit I've ever heard, young man. You expect to get away with that weak-ass story?" Scratch a spit-shined general deep enough and you inevitably get to a real human being.

"Yep. Can you prove otherwise?"

Murphy swiveled and looked at the officers to his left and right, but all he got for the effort were raised eyebrows. "Mr.—"

"Duffy," I reminded him.

"Mr. Duffy, listen up. I don't care what we can prove or not prove. Somebody's playing games, and I won't stand for it. I may not be able to nail you this time, but you people keep playing fast and loose with the rules and I'll skin you alive. Do you read me?"

"Affirmative, General." Politeness seemed to be the safest course of action. For their part, Nasser and his colonel sat wordlessly, more than willing, it seemed, to let me take all the heat.

Murphy nodded. "Good. At least we understand each other. Now, if you people would spend as much time training these soldiers as you have trying to beat the system, you might not be in the boat you're in. Take my advice, gentlemen, do it the honest way. It may take longer, but it'll pay off in the end."

"Yeah," Nasser said under his breath, "for U.S. Army Missile Command."

"What was that, Major?" Murphy's head jerked up from the papers he was studying.

I put a cautioning hand on Nasser's arm.

"Nothing, General. Absolutely nothing."

The three of us stood and headed straight for the door. Once outside, I turned to Nasser. "You guys go ahead. I've got some business to handle here."

Nasser's eyebrows raised.

"Kirby Benson," I answered the unspoken query.

Nasser nodded. "Look, Duffy," Nasser began. "We know that you've been stuck in a bad situation. Don't think we don't appreciate your handling things."

In other circumstances, I would have been touched. But this wasn't other circumstances, and these two guys had helped create the situation I was taking the heat for. "Thanks, guys. I appreciate that. But how about leaning on the boys to study a little harder?"

Nasser laughed. "Are you crazy? Every time I do that, I get a hundred parents at the front gate complaining that I'm mistreating their sons. We don't have an air force yet, Duffy. What we have is a glorified Cub Scout troop. But we're working on it."

I walked back to the main reception area outside Marine Post One and picked up the telephone. A voice came on in seconds. "May I help you?"

"L. Bruce Dalrymple, please."

"Just a second."

"Dalrymple."

"Bruce, this is Duffy. You wanted to see me today."

The pause on the other end confirmed that my pleasantries weren't appreciated. "I'll be right out."

I stayed on the line, waving at the operator behind the bulletproof glass.

"Hanks."

"Harvey, this is Duffy. You said to call you before I met with Dalrymple."

"Duffy, how they hanging?"

"Not great, Harvey. My roommate is still dead. I've spent the last half hour being berated by a U.S. Army general—"

"Quentin Murphy?"

"Roger that, Harvey. Now, I get to face down the inimitable L. Bruce Dalrymple."

"But not by yourself, Duffy, my boy. I've cleared my calendar just for you."

His words actually comforted me. It was right then that I knew I was crossing that razor-thin line between sanity and insanity, going in the wrong direction. That I could be comforted by the support of Harvey Hanks sent my belief in an ordered universe into terminal spiral.

Entering the conference room again, I plopped down into the chair recently occupied by General Murphy. L. Bruce Dalrymple stood beside me for a second, obviously disgruntled at my choice of seats, but he finally wandered to another chair. Harvey chuckled as he found a seat for himself.

"Mr. Duffy, I need to ask you some questions concerning the death of Kirby Benson. It is my responsibility to prepare a complete report for the ambassador, which will, in turn, allow the State Department to provide detailed information to Mr. Benson's family." Dalrymple produced a tape recorder, pressed a button, and sat back with an irritating smile.

"That's nice, Bruce."

A beautiful shade of crimson climbed up L. Bruce's neck. Harvey even smiled. "Mr. Duffy, this is a serious matter."

"You're damned right, Bruce. I'm the one who found Kirby floating in the Persian Gulf, remember?"

"Yes, well, that's true. Now, are you aware of any enemies that Mr. Benson might have had?" Something about the way Bruce asked the question made me think he didn't really care about the answer.

"Try everybody on the Patriot missile contract."

"Say again."

"Nobody liked him, Bruce. Nobody. He was an obnoxious creature. Thought he was a big-time writer. Kept telling me he was closing in on a big cover-up dealing with Gulf War Syndrome. But nobody I know, and that includes me, would waste a bullet to kill him."

L. Bruce and Harvey exchanged a glance, a brief, tell-all glance. I got the distinct impression that they had already discussed this topic at length.

"Mr. Duffy, I think it would be wise if you avoided mentioning Mr. Benson's unfortunate delusions. You'll just end up besmirching his memory."

"Look, Bruce. I'm just a poor old country boy. Why don't you translate that for me?"

"You ain't got no horse in this race, Duff," Harvey offered. "You go talking about Kirby's big story and people won't be saying 'poor Kirby.' They'll be saying 'poor moron Kirby.'"

L. Bruce leaned across the table with a frown etching its way across his face. "Let me spell it out for you, Mr. Duffy. Leave it alone. Benson's dead. Somebody killed him. That somebody is still out there. Don't stand in line to be next. We'll handle everything from this end." L. Bruce jerked upright, snatched his recorder, and stomped out of the room.

Chubby Harvey chuckled. "He's right about one thing, Duffy. Leave it alone. We'll get to the bottom of Benson's murder sooner or later. In the meantime, I'd rather not find *you* floating in the Gulf."

"Whatever you say, Harvey. I just want everything to get back to normal."

Harvey grinned. "What the hell's normal in Kuwait? Complete disbelief is the best policy." He stood. "Have a good lunch and just put all this behind you. I'll keep Bruce off your back. But if this Abdulmohsen character shows up, give me a call. And don't believe all that shit you hear about Karen notching her bra strap with her male conquests. Rumors like that are usually started by people she wouldn't bang."

"What do you do around here, Harvey?"

Old Harvey just grinned. "Let's say I keep an eye on things for Uncle Sam."

"Do I read that 'spook'?"

"Don't read it at all. Just consider me your friend."

At that point, I needed all the friends I could get. "You got it, Harve. You're about the only one here who's treated me decent."

"Don't forget that if things get hairy." He stopped and checked his watch.

I held back. "Harvey, since I've been in this country, I've been inundated with nut cases, opium addicts, alcoholic diplomats and scheming Arabs. Isn't there something wrong with that picture?"

Harvey shrugged. "Not in Kuwait."

"Am I supposed to find some solace in that?"

"Reality," Harvey intoned, "rarely offers solace. Just remember, Duffy, if the bullets start flying, never move in a straight line. Serpentine. Serpentine."

CHAPTER
SIXTEEN

I experienced the strangest feeling as I sat down with Karen in the embassy cafeteria: this was a woman I didn't want to lose. I mean, I could give you a big line about her brown hair framing her face, the mischievous curve of her mouth when she smiled, the soft glow emanating from her as we touched hands. But that would all be secondary.

The simple truth was, I knew I loved her. Just like you know that if you stay up long enough, sooner or later the sun will come up. I decided right then that if I was going to keep Karen, I had to let her in on everything. Serge. Marina. Kirby. Farwaniya. Keeping secrets from the one you love is the surest path to a failed relationship.

"You look like you've had a rough day. Want to tell me about it?"

I poked a fork in the microwave-heated lasagna, twisted it aimlessly, and started talking. Frank. Benson and his story of the century. Serge and Marina. Nasser and crew. For the first time I didn't hold anything back. She didn't say a word as I wrapped up the epic, just gave out a nervous chuckle and picked at her chicken curry, as microwaved to perfection as my own.

"Duffy, you're an incredible guy. The fact that all these people have centered on you says that. But you don't want to get caught between Harvey and Dalrymple. Harvey's, well, Harvey's just Harvey. But Dalrymple believes in the slash and burn school of diplomacy. I think he missed his calling."

"Yeah? What was that?"

"Totalitarian leader of a totalitarian state, subjugating the populace with whips and chains."

I nodded. "The Allen Dulles School."

"With distance learning from the J. Edgar Hoover Academy. We're joking about all this, but I'm serious, Duffy. You need to stay as far away from these people as possible, especially Sergei Malenkov. He's big trouble. Word on the dip circuit is that he's just on the edge of being recalled."

"That's funny. He claims he's just on the edge of being named an ambassador. Is he a drunk? Of course. But then I haven't met a sober Russian. Maybe it's something in the water."

"Why do you persist in turning everything into a joke?"

"It's a southern thing. But what I said was true. I *have* never seen a sober Russian."

Karen giggled. "You may be right." The smile disappeared. "Promise that you'll stay away from those bozos."

I stuffed a forkful of lasagna in my mouth and chewed thoughtfully.

"Duffy?"

"My daddy always told me not to make promises I knew I couldn't keep."

"Duffy!"

"Karen. I promised Serge that I would find out what his daughter was up to. In the process of fulfilling that promise, I saw my roommate hustled by two gorillas. That spells kidnapping to me. Anyway, the next day, I find this dearly despised roommate floating in the Persian Gulf with a bullet hole where his forehead used to be. Next, Happy Harvey and Butthole Bruce take an unnatural interest in me, advising me that I should seek my entertainment elsewhere. This all adds up to a pile shoulder-high. I don't want to end up on the bottom of the pile."

About that time, old L. Bruce himself wandered into the cafeteria, stopping long enough to spot me with Karen and frown his disgust. Karen didn't miss it either. She leaned forward conspiratorily. "See what I mean. I'll probably get a call from him later."

"Yeah? About what?"

"My efficiency reports. My job performance."

"What the hell does he do around here?"

"He's the DCM, the deputy chief of mission. Consider him like the assistant ambassador. And he's the terror of the dip staff."

"Harvey doesn't seem too scared of him."

"Harvey wouldn't. Don't you know what he does?"

"All Harvey would tell me is that he keeps an eye on things for Uncle Sam."

She lowered her head and whispered, "He's the CIA station chief."

"Well, I didn't think he was a used-car salesman, although that was my second choice." I stopped for a second. "Why do I get the feeling that you trust the CIA station chief more than the deputy chief of mission? Isn't there something wrong with this picture?" I looked at Karen with true confusion.

"What most people don't know is that earlier in his career, Bruce was loaned out to the national security advisor's office and, somehow, became a card-carrying national intelligence officer. Unfortunately for Bruce, his career in the NSA office was cut short by the resignation of his boss, Admiral Thomas Poindexter, of Iran-Contra fame. Bruce still considers himself something of an intelligence hotshot, and I guess to a certain extent he is, but rumor has it that he's about as effective an intelligence officer as he is a DCM. I hear he likes to stick his nose in Harvey's business. Harvey dislikes interference, and since technically, Harvey doesn't work for the State Department, he has a certain freedom that the rest of us don't enjoy."

"Is Harvey good at what he does?"

"Word has it that he's one of the best around, unlike Bruce Dalrymple."

"I'll promise you this," I said, forking down the last bite of lasagna. "I'll stay away from L. Bruce if he'll stay away from me."

"That wasn't quite the commitment I had in mind."

I certainly didn't want to piss her off. But at that point, I wasn't willing to promise anything. It was patently obvious that L. Bruce, the DCM, had invited me to the embassy merely to deliver his barely veiled threat. I don't like being threatened. Call me stupid, call me strange, call me a redneck. I'll probably answer to all those, but I don't like being jerked around, and I wasn't going to leave them alone until they left me alone.

"Look," I said finally. "I should probably be getting back to the base. You know, the 'earn-my-daily-bread' routine."

"Okay," she conceded. "But call me later, when you get home. And Duffy? *Try* to stay out of trouble."

Pulling back out on the Maghreb and heading south toward the air base, I noticed a white Caprice Classic following me.

Caprice Classics are as thick on the Kuwaiti roads as watermelons on the Fourth of July. They're built like tanks and handle desert weather better than Land Rovers. Just about every Kuwaiti household has one. But this car wasn't driven by a Kuwaiti. A Westerner was in the driver's seat, and he seemed remarkably interested in me and my car.

Something about being followed as I left my own embassy, where my roommate's murder was the topic of the day, didn't sit well. I decided to find out whether I was just being paranoid. I pulled a fast one and slid off the exit for the air base at the last possible second. Checking my rear view, I watched as the Caprice slammed into a fishtail, careening past the exit with smoking, squealing tires. Then, in true Kuwaiti tradition, the driver threw the gears in reverse and backed up the highway to make the turn he'd missed as I trundled down the road to the base, and as I turned onto the road to the base's main gate, I saw the Caprice slow down and park.

This was not good, but for the life of me, I didn't know exactly what to do.

I pulled into the parking lot beside the school and saw Jack sitting on a bench just outside the main door, his bald head propped up in his hands. Visions of another heart flutter immediately came to mind, and I slammed the car door.

"Oh, Duffy, tell me the truth. Did somebody really shoot Kirby Benson in the head?"

"Yeah, Jack. Somebody did."

"But why, Duffy?"

"I guess he got in somebody's way, Jack."

"Are we still in trouble with the embassy about the ECL?"

"How did you know about that?"

He waved a wrinkled hand. "Oh, nothing stays secret for very long with this crew." He reached over and patted my knee. There was something, I don't know, paternal in the way he did it. "Be careful, Duffy. I've known Frank for a long, long time. He seems to just drift in and out of these projects, and I've never seen him handle one competently. He's always drunk or high or something. If Frank ever sobers up long enough to figure out how competent you are, he'll make life miserable for you. Competence frightens him. He knows he doesn't have anything to fear from me or most of the others. But you're different. Just watch your step."

"I will. Thanks, Jack."

At that moment, George ran out of the office, hopping from one foot to the other, his mustache awiggle. "Boss! Boss!"

Somehow, I half-expected him to go, "Zee plane! Zee plane, Boss!" But, alas, my nostalgia for *Fantasy Island* was not to be satisfied. "Major Nasser inside." My own personal ball and chain.

"Major! Long time no see. How are you?" I smiled in an appropriately smart-ass way.

The dapper major lit a cigarette and blew smoke. "Duffy, that was a magnificent performance today. But you and I both know that our problem isn't going to stop with General Murphy."

"Of course not, Major. We're just fighting a delaying action." I stopped and looked out the window at the parade ground. "But if you people hadn't screwed with the answer keys, we wouldn't be in this mess."

Nasser laughed long and deep. "Duffy, Duffy. You have the balls of a lion." He dropped into one of the swivel chairs. "You're right, though. We got greedy and put ourselves in this situation. You can be assured that it won't happen again. The problem now is how to get General Murphy off our asses. Make no mistake, Duffy. That's not a wish, that's a demand."

I nodded. "Leave it with me for a day or two. We've got that much time anyway. I'll think of something." I paused. "Tell me something, Major. Why didn't you go running to Frank with this thing? I mean, he collaborated with you to begin with."

Nasser nodded. "It's true. But, you see, Duffy, Frank is easily manipulated. He is not, however, a manipulator. You have a devious mind, Duffy. I knew from the beginning that you were my kind of guy."

"Why am I not comforted by that?"

Nasser lit a cigarette and inhaled deeply. "When this is all over, Duffy, get out of Kuwait. Go back to the U.S. You're a good guy. You deserve a normal life."

Didn't *anybody* think Kuwait was normal?

With Nasser's advice floating in my ears, I finished out the day by staying pretty much to myself. Fitzy was engrossed in the *New York Times* crossword. Perry was, well, I wasn't sure where Perry was, but I avoided the men's latrine, especially when I saw that little Mohammed was nowhere to be found, either.

Normally, I would have offered Jack or one of the other guys a ride back, but that bunch always hit the officers' mess before going home. The mess kept this incredible buffet going most of the time with spices so heavy I could smell them in my sweat. My pants didn't fit after my first trip there, so I backed off on the buffet. Anyway, with my own personal watchdog probably still outside the gates, I figured it wasn't polite to drag anybody else into my troubles.

About a hundred yards past the guard shack, I could see sunlight reflect off the familiar white Caprice Classic. Since the Caprice seemed happy to just follow me, I quit worrying and drove straight home. The security guards were kicked back, pleasantly snoring, oblivious to anything except the insides of their eyelids. Back home, we've got some pretty stiff penalties for sleeping on duty. In Kuwait, they give out commendations just for showing up.

CHAPTER
SEVENTEEN

With Kirby gone, Frank decided not to give me another roommate, a perk, I guess, of being a senior instructor. So, I could help myself to Kirby's stock of wine and crash on the couch. It was a simple pleasure, modest in its demands, satisfying in its rewards. Sheltered in the softness of its cushions, I could forget about Nasser, Frank, General Murphy, Kirby, Serge, and all the other assorted little demons of Kuwait.

For about five minutes. Somebody starting lightly tapping at the door. I almost didn't answer it. I almost turned back over and went back to sleep. Ignorant and naive as I am, I crawled off the couch and opened the door. I didn't even look out the peephole. Anybody who would tap that softly couldn't be an inmate of my Kuwaiti zoo.

"Duffy! My friend!" And I was engulfed once again by Serge's massive arms, crushed against his chest while he squeezed every bit of oxygen from my lungs.

"Serge—how—about—letting—go?"

He released me and I collapsed to the floor one more time. Serge started pacing back and forth, wringing his pudgy hands and slicking back his blond hair. "Duffy, you have news for me, news of my Marina?"

"I know where she is, Serge," I admitted, finally catching my breath. Serge's greetings were becoming hazardous to my health.

"Duffy!" The voice came from the door, and I remembered, too late, that I forgot to shut it. Karen stood, with hands on hips, in the doorway. "Don't!"

"Jesus, Karen! How about a little warning?"

"Stay out of it, Duffy. This is his problem." She jerked her head toward Serge.

"Duffy, what does she know about Marina? You should not have told her!" His face grew red and I thought he was going to go ballistic.

"Karen! You're creating a real shitstorm for me here."

"Duffy, don't accuse me of creating a shitstorm. You're the rainmaker, pal. But if you get caught in all this, I can't save you."

"Who asked you to?" The old Tennessee pride reared its ugly head.

"Duffy!" This from Karen.

"Duffy!" This from Serge.

I felt like a husband with two wives.

"Serge, buddy, it's like this. Karen knows everything. There's nothing you or I can do about that, so get over it. Karen, whether you like it or not, I promised Serge that I'd keep an eye on his daughter, and I don't go back on my promises. And that's all I'm gonna say. Get that?" I said as forcefully as I could.

She took a step back and blinked.

Serge took a step forward and slapped me on the back, almost sending me crashing to the floor again. "*Walla*, I trust your judgment, Duffy! What have you found out?"

"Well, Serge," I answered, avoiding the look of disbelief on Karen's face, and trying like hell to figure out how much to tell Serge and what, exactly, to hold back. "It's like this—"

"Heyyyyy, ya'llllll!"

I shivered in my sneakers. Only one person in Kuwait talked like that, besides me that is. One of these days, I really *would* learn to close my door. There she stood—the ever-available Debbie.

"Welllll, heeyyy, Duffy! Ain't you gonna introduce me to your friends?" And Debbie staggered into the apartment. Obviously, she was well on her way to a new kind of high.

I just rubbed my eyes and made a slow half-turn. "Debbie, Karen and Serge. Karen and Serge, Debbie." After all, what else could I do?

"Where's Kirby?" Debbie made herself right at home, heading for a cabinet I'd never opened and pulling out candles.

"Debbie," I intoned as solemnly as I could with Karen's eyes burning holes in me, "Kirby's dead."

That, at least, got her attention. She looked up from lighting the candles and frowned. "Bummer. Ahh was gonna get him to pay me for some more talkin'. Easiest money I ever made ceptin' on my back. You ain't got any hash, do you?"

"Who's she?" Karen's tone was somewhere between a stiletto and one of those Ginsu knives they advertise on TV.

"I've told you about her," I started, but I could tell by her face that she was choosing not to remember that part of my tale. "It's a long story. She's . . ."

"Ah'm a friend of Duffy's. Who the fuck are youuu?" Debbie obviously wasn't wasted enough to miss Karen's tone.

"I'm out of here," Karen said, swiveling toward the door.

"Karen!" I lunged and grabbed her arm. "Please, give me a chance to explain!"

"Duffy!" Serge pleaded.

"Not now, Serge!"

"Duffy!" Debbie whined.

"Put a sock in it, Debbie!"

Karen stopped. "You better have one hell of an explanation," she said, glowering at me.

"Just sit down for a second." So, Karen stomped over to a chair and plopped down. I turned back to my own gruesome twosome.

"Serge, I know where Marina is. I'll take care of it." Short, sweet, and to the point.

"Debbie, Kirby's dead and I don't have time go into the details, and I don't have any hash. Why don't you go . . . do . . . something . . ." I paused.

"You will go and bring her back to me?" Serge begged.

"No, Duffy!" Karen said, rising from the chair.

"Yes, Serge. Now, go do something. Go find Linna. Go get laid. Anything, just let me handle this."

"Heyyy," Debbie began, sidling up to Serge. "You wanna fuck? I know just the place. C'mon," and she took his ever-present Stoli from him and turned it up.

Serge snatched the bottle back and nodded at me. "Okay. I will trust you. I go with her now."

Running off with Debbie wasn't quite what I'd had in mind for Serge, but who was I to argue? The three of them, Serge, Debbie, and the Stoli bottle, disappeared out the door.

"Where's my explanation?" Karen demanded.

I told her about the Caprice on my tail. "Baby, it's gotten too screwed up for me to bail out now. I've got a feeling that if I don't figure out what's really going on with Kirby's death, I may not live to make it home. Kirby sure as hell didn't. And it all seems to center on that villa in Farwaniya."

"I hate to admit it, but you've got a point," Karen conceded.

"What I need right now are some special forces boys, or James Bond or something. Hell, I'd settle for Nat and Franz . . ."

"Who are Nat and Franz?"

But I didn't answer, because that proverbial lightbulb blazed to life in my brain. I grabbed the phone and punched some numbers from memory.

"What are you doing, Duffy?"

I held up a hand as a sleepy voice reached out from the receiver.

"Brian, my boy. How are you?"

"Duffy? What the fuck's wrong with you, mate? Don't you know I take my nap every day about now?"

"Sorry, Brian, but I didn't get a copy of your weekly schedule. This will only take a minute. Remember telling me about that high-class whorehouse in Farwaniya?"

"Aye."

"Where is it?"

"What's wrong, mate? Karen cut you off?" And he described the location.

And just as I thought, it was the villa that I'd seen Marina walk into and Kirby Benson dragged into.

"Why all the interest?" Brian asked, suddenly at least three-quarters serious.

"Just a little company business," I said, sounding more sinister than I intended.

"Look, Duffy, don't be getting yourself into a cock-up. It ain't so easy to get out of over here. Ring me up if you get your ass flapping in the wind."

"Later." And I hung up, gnawing my lower lip as all the cylinders began to click into place.

"So, how was your hunch?" Karen asked.

"Dead on. We've got a stop to make later." I figured to slip in, get Marina, and get out. No fuss. No muss.

"We've got a stop to make now. The commercial counselor is having a little get-together at his place and we're invited. If we don't show up, then somebody'll mention it."

Cleaning up was composed of showering and shaving off my beard and mustache. My mother always advised me to be clean-cut if I was going to get killed. "You don't want to have people finding you all scruffy-looking," she cautioned me. "And wear clean underwear."

~ ~ ~

Obviously, I was in the wrong business. The C.C.'s villa made me terminally ill. Posh wasn't the word. Let's try luxurious. How about suitable for *Lifestyles of the Rich and Famous*? The walls were covered in Persian carpets; apparently no one had heard about the trade sanctions against Iran. A pair of satanic Mau-Mau masks dangled on wires suspended from the ceiling. A bar stretched across the back wall, and a trio of Filipinos in red and black jackets waited patiently for the onslaught of diplomatic drunks.

We had driven Karen's car. The Caprice had been sitting in the gravel parking lot behind the Marhaba Complex, but with the super-tinted windows in Karen's car, my personal shadows just gave us a cursory glance and turned back to the apartment building.

Thirty minutes later, I found myself in the living room making small talk with the Venezuelan ambassador.

"But you see, Mr. Duffy, things are not well at all for me here." He shook his head sadly and leaned toward me conspiratorially. "I tell you in confidence, Mr. Duffy, I spend most of my time signing condolence books for all these interminable Sabahs who keep dying. Otherwise, I sit in my office and drink tea."

"Not much happening on the trade front, huh?"

"No, and I'm afraid it will remain so. I tried once to sell some excess rice we had, but the Kuwaitis can get it so much cheaper from India and Pakistan. Another time I offered oil well parts, but again France provides the same item at half the cost. I confess, were it not for OPEC I would not be here at all."

Just as I started looking for an escape hatch, I saw the front door open and two men walk in. My heart dropped down around my ankles as I recognized one of the two; he had dragged Kirby into the villa in Farwaniya.

It took about five minutes, but I finally found Karen looking for a plant to ditch her drink in.

"We've got to go," I whispered, grabbing her by the elbow and steering her toward the door.

I pointed at my favorite pair of kidnappers and leaned close to her ear. "The big one, my dear, is the guy who drove Kirby Benson to Farwaniya."

Karen turned pale and shook her head. "No, Duffy, don't say that."

"Why?"

"Look who they're talking to."

I followed her finger and nodded sagely to myself at the insanity of it all. Heckle and Jeckle were engaged in deep conversation with the Honorable L. Bruce Dalrymple, and from the looks of it, they were all very well acquainted.

"If they're going to the same place we're going, I'd just as soon get there and leave before they show up," Karen said.

"Sound advice. I knew there was a reason I loved you."

And then I realized I'd said the "L" word. The funny thing was, I didn't mind. Hell, I'd go further than that. I *liked* the idea.

She smiled. "We damned well better get out of this caper alive, 'cause I'm gonna hold you to it."

We made the drive to Farwaniya in record time, leaving only three head-on collisions in our wake, which was fewer than the average Kuwaiti caused on his way to work. Short of breaking the sound barrier, there was no way that the Dynamic Duo could beat us to the villa, but I laid down on the accelerator anyway. No future in making assumptions.

We scanned the front of the villa. Quiet. No guards. No watchmen. I figured the gatekeepers were inside, checking on the scene from elevated positions. I glanced at the rooftops of the villas on either side. It took a second, but I finally saw the shadows drifting along the moon-brightened skyline. One thing about Kuwait, cloudy nights were rare; you could always count on a certain amount of moonlight.

I figured the boys on the roof would only react if they saw something out of the ordinary, so I acted as stuffy as I could. Hey, this place catered to the diplomatic crowd; I would just fit in.

It worked. The closest shadow paused at the roofline for the briefest of seconds and then moved on his appointed rounds.

I left Karen behind and slipped through the gate. Light filtered out of the heavily curtained front windows and scattered a zebra pattern across the walk.

The walkway slid between shoulder-high walls and funneled the visitor straight into the front door. No chance of straying off the beaten path. My eyes roved around the villa's three-story white facade as I finished the short trek from gate to door. The courtyard interior was marbled and a set of stairs led down to a basement entrance directly below the front door. I picked out the camera covering the basement door quickly; it was secured to the overhang beneath the front steps, pointed down to the descending stairway.

If there was a camera covering the basement door, the front door and courtyard were on somebody's surveillance screen too. Finally, I locked on them. Two dark little boxes nestled under the eaves of the building. Security cameras. Someone knew exactly who was coming in and going out. I figured that somewhere in the wall was a cleverly disguised metal detector. The bad guys might even know my social security number.

Glancing back over my shoulder, I hoped for a last look at Karen before I stepped into the abyss. But, alas, the walls blocked my view. So much for one of those long, lingering, soulful stares as I kept my date with destiny. Strangely enough, I wasn't panicking. Until I got to the door, that is. And I stared at the doorbell blankly. What if there was a password? I had forgotten to ask Brian about that little detail.

CHAPTER
EIGHTEEN

So, there I stood, outside Heidi Fleiss's dream house looking at the doorbell like it was the release trigger for a cyanide pellet. I did the reasonable thing and knocked on the door.

And, lo and behold, it opened.

A smiling Filipino, dressed in the ubiquitous red and black jacket, just like the bartenders at embassy parties, appeared in the doorway. Must be some kind of national uniform.

"Oh, I say, 'allo there." My British accent was decidedly phony, but since that was my best bet, I figured, what the hell?

"May I help you?" he asked in amazingly unaccented English.

Think fast, Duffy. Really fast. "Uhhh, hummh, I'm Farnsley Beesworth, new first secretary at the British Embassy. A certain Captain O'Neill suggested that I might be able to find some, well, ummh, 'diversion' here. If you take my drift, I mean."

But, rather than laugh and slam the door in my face, the Filipino simply smiled even wider. "Of course, sir. Please, come in. Captain O'Neill is one of our best customers."

Best customer, huh? I couldn't wait to get my hands on Brian, and a barrage of possible insults came to mind as the guy led me into an ornately decorated parlor. Very Western in appearance, although more Victorian than modern, actually. A pair of major league couches sat against one wall, looking oddly like something from a furniture store clearance sale, you know, the thousand-dollar couches with flowers and mystery stains.

"If you'll have a seat, I'll bring some of the ladies by for your approval. Do you have any special requests?" This guy could give lessons in whorehouse etiquette.

"Rather sparse attendance, wouldn't you say?" I grumbled, glancing around and seeing nobody.

My Filipino major domo just continued to smile. "You and another gentleman are our only guests at the moment. Our patrons don't usually arrive this early. For the completely discreet visitor, we also have private entrances through the rear."

"How utterly thoughtful of you. Something in a blond, I think."

The little fellow actually leered. "Of course. Would you like to choose for yourself, or should I use my judgment?"

"I'd rather do it myself. Do many people just take, potluck, I believe the Yanks call it?"

"A few rely on our good taste," and he disappeared through a door.

I settled in for a few minutes' break. The way I had it figured, by ordering a blond, I had a decent shot at getting Marina. She might recognize me, but I had even money that she wouldn't. On the one or two times we'd met, she'd paid me all the attention she'd give an empty shoebox. My contingency plan? I'd get my girl upstairs and then I'd rummage through the rooms until I found Marina, or until the bouncer found *me*. Once I got my hands on her, maybe she could shed some light on the Kirby Benson mess. Maybe not. But it was my best shot.

I followed my personal pimp into a long, narrow room with a window running the length of one wall; he motioned toward a narrow, cushioned bench. "Please."

I felt like I was watching a police lineup. In seconds, three young blonds wandered into the chamber beyond the window—two females and a male. How customer-oriented, I thought. Neither one of the females was Marina. The second one, though, looked an awful lot like the girl who had climbed into the Mercedes with her at the aerobics studio. "I'll take her," I said.

We walked down a hallway to a set of stairs at the back of the villa. A door set in the rear wall looked like the back entrance my host had mentioned. I made a mental note of it. Back doors always seem to come in handy.

My heart was thumping loud enough to trigger a seismograph. If Marina was here, where was she? The Filipino pimp said there was one other guy here. Maybe he'd picked Marina. Maybe not.

"We would have had more choices for you," my guide explained as we mounted the stairs, "but our other patron also favors blonds, and brunettes as well."

"Quite," I said magnanimously.

He led me down a long hallway with many doors, all cracked open except one, at the very end of the hall. The Filipino pushed the door fully open. "You may relax in here. Your companion will join you in a few moments. The small refrigerator has a fully stocked bar if you would like some refreshment."

And then he was gone. And I was standing in the middle of the room with a hooker on the way and absolutely no interest in that kind of performance.

What the hell do I do now? "Piss-poor prior planning," my daddy would have said. "You're the only boy I know," he'd say, "that could spend the night in a whorehouse and not get laid." But then came a rustling at the door, and the blond came in wearing nothing but a smile and a pair of saggy breasts, and when she said, "Me love you long time," I knew she'd been watching too many American movies.

Her eyes were glassy, the pupils more like little dots than living flesh. This honey had obviously been smoking too much wacky weed, and I wasn't sure I could trust anything she told me.

"Come here," I said.

Obedient as a little robot, she came.

"Sit." I indicated the bed.

That command she understood. She sat, lay back, and spread her legs.

"Sit up. I want to talk to you."

Her eyes narrowed—well, at least as much as they could— and she said, "*Shinoo hadha?*" What is this? Great, I thought. She can't even tell the difference between Tennessee redneck and Arab.

"*Kellum Anglaise?*" Survival Arabic at its best. "Do you speak English?"

"*Da.*"

I love Kuwait. Absurdity at its finest. I'm having a conversation in Arabic with a Russian prostitute. "Where's Marina?"

"*Minoo?*" Who?

"Marina."

"Marina?"

"Marina! *Da!*" I figured what the hell, throw a little Russian at her. Couldn't hurt.

She shook her head. "No. I better Marina."

Then I heard the gunshot, muffled though it was, from down the hall.

I think it was the fear in my little slut's eyes that did the trick. The second giveaway, I guess, was when I heard a scream. Leaving blondie naked on the bed, I sprinted out the door toward the sound of the screaming.

You're probably asking yourself why a reasonably sane man would run toward the sound of violence in a whorehouse? Because absurdly, I was still trying to save Serge's daughter. For all I knew, she was the one doing the screaming. Call it a gift, call it luck, call it any damned thing you want, but I was right.

Unfortunately, Serge himself lay on the bed with half his head splattered over the sheets and a nasty-looking pistol in his hand. Debbie sat upright in the bed, the sheet piled up in her lap, staring at the big, red hole in Serge's head. Marina, stark-naked, stood in shock before him, screaming like a refugee from *The Blair Witch Project*.

Poor Serge. You couldn't help but like the guy, despite his drunken antics. I could only guess at the shock of finding out that your concerns about your daughter were even worse than you imagined. Once you got past all the other stuff—all the diplomatic, alcoholic Russian baloney—he had been, finally, just a father worried about his little girl.

Footsteps pounding down the hallway brought something resembling my wits back, and I grabbed Marina's hand. "C'mon! We've got to get out of here!" I figured that Debbie could fend for herself, and for some reason, I felt like I owed it to Serge.

"NO!" the naked beauty answered, refusing to move an inch.

"It's that English teacher son of a bitch!" I heard a voice behind me say.

I chanced a look over my shoulder and sure enough, my luck was holding. Kirby Benson's last escorts came at me with pistols the size of rocket launchers in hand.

I was facing a major decision. Die like a man; run like a coward; pray for rain.

I said to no one in particular, "Cannon to the left of them; cannon to the right; cannon in front of them volley'd and thunder'd; Storm'd at with shot and shell, Boldly they rode and well, Into the jaws of Death, Into the mouth of Hell, Rode the six hundred . . ."

A cannonball slapped into my shoulder. And as I started to fall, I heard one of the two men yell loud and clear. "NO! He said to take him alive!"

I wished to hell I'd known that before I started my Light Brigade reenactment. And that was the last thing I thought as darkness closed in.

CHAPTER
NINETEEN

"**W**ho the hell are you?" The voice drifted from beyond the bright light, in the shadows of a room I couldn't define. Faces floated lazily in the darkness, globes of white in a room without lights. Sort of reminded me of jack-o-lanterns, but Halloween was long gone and far away.

My shoulder hurt like hell, and from the trickle of blood running down my temple, I figured if I made it to morning, I'd have a headache as big as Saddam Hussein's ego. I couldn't decide whether answering their questions gave me a better chance of survival, or if refusing to cooperate would.

I opted for cooperation. "Edward James Duffy. You want my serial number?"

"Who do you work for?" A new voice chipped in, this one with a clear British accent.

"Arthur Watson, Incorporated, of Providence, Rhode Island. You already know all this; why don't you just get to the point?"

"Who do you really work for? Don't give us any bullshit answers!" My American interrogator jabbed a heavy finger into my shoulder and pain shot through me, rattling torn nerves, and I felt bile geysering up. "What's your connection to Sergei Malenkov?"

"Look," I sputtered. "I was just doing a favor for him, a favor for a friend."

"Very commendable," said another voice, floating in from the darkness. But this voice I knew, and I didn't have the slightest idea how he was involved, and that scared the hell out of me. "I'd think I was in the presence of fucking Mahatma Gandhi, Duffman, if I didn't know better." And then a face joined the voice, moving into the bouncing glow of the single, bare bulb, hanging from the ceiling.

"Frank! You're sober."

And sure enough, it was good old Frank Crawford, the Patriot project manager. Old Frank, the hash-smoking lush. Frank, the obscenity-spewing, never-drew-a-sober-breath poster child for ethanol abuse. But this Frank was different; no bleariness in these eyes, and those thin chicken lips were stretched taut across his face.

"Cute, Duffman. Cute." He circled me and eased himself in a chair. The others hovered at the edge of my reality.

My shoulder was killing me, but my new playmates had patched me up enough to stop the bleeding.

"You're almost as big a pain in the ass, Duffman, as Kirby Benson."

"Coming from you, I consider that a compliment."

For a second, I thought I saw anger flash in Frank's eyes, just a quick burst of lightning, but then they shut off expression, like a hooded cobra. "It was a great plan. Too bad you won't be around to see your country profit from it."

"Our countries," corrected that supercilious British twit hiding in the corner.

"What is this place?" I said, glancing around.

"A deserted palace. Belonged to one of the emir's ancestors. The Iraqis used it for a prison. This room," and Frank tapped lovingly on the wall, "was one of their torture chambers."

"Where's Karen? Where's Marina?" I knew they had them.

"Tucked away," Frank assured me. "I needed to find out how much you knew before I made any decisions."

"And?" I figured it was too late to worry about getting fired for insubordination.

"And," he said with a smile. "You get the pleasure of dying in the service of your country; we'll frame Benson's pal Abdulmohsen and use it to drive a wedge between Kuwait and Iran. And your girlfriend will end up as another casualty of the dangerous Kuwaiti highways. The concept, Duffy, is called 'terminate with extreme prejudice'."

"Thanks for clarifying." I was thinking fast. Had to stall for time. Had to. The longer I stayed alive, the more chance I could keep all of us alive. Granted, I was tied to a chair with a hole in my shoulder, but hope, Stephen King tells us, is a good thing. Think!

"Hey, Frank. Since I'm giving my life for this unknown cause, you want to explain exactly what I'm dying for?" As long as I kept him talking, I stayed alive. The others were quiet; only the sound of their feet shuffling across the dusty floor reminded me they were still there.

His eyes sort of glazed over and I knew I had him. "It's a stroke of brilliance actually. A place like Kuwait is tailor-made for something like this operation. You've got all these diplomats crammed into this tiny little country. The Emirates were already crowded with Russian hookers, so we just imported some here, with the assistance of our British colleagues from MI6."

"And recruited locally, it would appear," I pointed out.

Frank allowed a half-frown to encroach on his smile. "That was the only fuck-up in an otherwise beautiful operation."

"I'd say that recruiting the daughter of the Russian consul as one of your hookers ought to rank right up there with the greatest fuck-ups of all time."

"By the time I realized what was going on, she was one of our best performers. The name of the game, Duffman, is bio and assessment. Collect as much biographical data as possible and then assess whether the targets can be compromised and turned into double agents. Men talk in bed. We had all the rooms wired. You'd be surprised at how many weren't too keen on having their own personal sex videos delivered to their governments. Amazing how they opened up to us."

Remarkable, I thought. "So, you ran a high-class whorehouse to compromise foreign diplomats."

"The human side of intelligence gathering, Duffman, has been sadly neglected of late. The CIA doesn't have the balls for this kind of thing anymore, so the NSA has to step into the trenches. Running these ESL programs is a perfect cover. They're so screwed you can get away with literal murder. Besides, with those ridiculous salaries they pay you pansies, the NSA was relieved of the burden of paying me. Let the Kuwaitis carry the freight."

"What about Benson? Why kill him?"

"While he fiddled around with his story of the century, somehow he stumbled across the Farwaniya operation, hooked up with that slut, Debbie. He became expendable." Frank shrugged with just the slightest hint of resignation. "Besides, he was getting too chummy with that Abdulmohsen character.

We deemed him a danger to national security. Anyway, I never liked faggots."

"So, if this is an NSA operation, can I presume that L. Bruce Dalrymple has his sticky fingers in it?" Just a few more seconds. I was trying to slip the rope over my thumb.

Frank straightened just a little. "Bruce Dalrymple is a true patriot. If we had more Dalrymples in this country, the world would be safe for democracy. The Tree of Liberty must be refreshed from time to time with the blood of patriots. Bruce Dalrymple said that."

"No, Frank. Thomas Jefferson said that. What about Malenkov?" Keep him talking.

"Malenkov came with Debbie, feeling pretty frisky, wanted a blond in a hurry for a threesome, and the Filipino pimp sent his daughter to him. The fucking Russkie gets all suicidal and blows his own brains out."

"That brings up another question." I had the thumb out. Almost there. "How are you going to explain away a dead Russian consul?"

"Simple. He committed suicide and that's the way it will be reported. Just not at the Farwaniya site."

I had a desperate urge to wrap my fingers around Frank's scrawny throat. If I could get my hands free. Two people were depending on me right then—Karen and Marina. And I was almost there. My wrists were raw from struggling against the ropes, and I felt a warm, sticky, wetness inching over my fingers. Then I felt it. Just a hint of slack that wasn't there before; and I knew I'd gotten loose. Or at least I thought I had.

Until yet another familiar voice sounded off. This time from the darkness behind me.

"Boys, readjust Mr. Duffy's rope. It seems to be a little loose."

"Brucie. Somehow, I knew you'd be around here somewhere."

Two of his men—the two who had so kindly put a hole in my shoulder—advanced on me. "You could have at least stopped me before I rubbed my wrists raw," I pouted. And why not? I was about to travel to that undiscovered country from whose bourne no travelers return; I could pout if I wanted to.

"Go ahead," counseled L. Bruce, as Frank smirked at me. "A dying man deserves the chance to speak his mind."

And then the light went out.

CHAPTER
TWENTY

"**W**hat the fuck!" Frank's voice was the first and loudest.

I couldn't see my hand in front of my face; and then I realized that I *had* my hand in front of my face. Oh, yeah! They never got around to retying me.

Somewhere in the darkness, I heard the unmistakable sound of fist hitting flesh, stomach it sounded like, and the resulting expulsion of air.

"OOOFF!"

"This way, mate," a friendly British voice whispered in my ear as a hand closed around my shoulder.

"What took you so damned long? They almost fed me to the camels."

"Later," Brian O'Neill of Her Majesty's Armed Forces suggested. "And you're a damned lucky sod that I decided to see what you were up to."

"No argument here. We've got to find Karen and Marina."

"Aye, you head out the door and go right. I'll confuse these lads a bit more and then head left. Go out the side door, by the old swimming pool, and my Land Rover's parked in the drive."

Fist thudded against flesh again.

"Who the fuck else is in here?" Frank shouted. As I felt my way out the door and into the wide, musty hallway, I heard Frank's shouts break into a suddenly higher pitch, about two octaves higher to be exact. Only one thing can cause a vocal range like that. Brian wasn't ignoring him.

A hint of moonlight slipped into the corridor, and after the pitch black of the room, it was like flipping a light switch. The damned corridor stretched forever, and to top that off, I saw a grand staircase at the far end. Jesus, the place was huge! Where, in an abandoned palace, would Frank and L. Bruce put two women? Behind me, it sounded like Brian was giving the boys all they could handle. So, when in doubt, scream.

"KAREN!"

"DUFFY!"

Homing in on the melodic sounds of Karen's screaming, I cut a trail down the corridor. Then, just when I thought I had her, I realized that there were three doors that could be harboring her. I kicked the hell out of Door #2.

Nothing but more darkness and more dust.

"Duffy! You moron! I'm in here."

Door #3. One more swift kick of the boot and my beloved lay revealed, or at least sat revealed, bedraggled and rumpled, and unmistakably pissed off.

"Duffy," she said, with even, careful words. "If we get out of this alive, I'm going to . . ."

"Kill me," I added helpfully as I tried to untie her.

"No. I'm going to marry you. Then, I'll kill you."

Back down the hall, a couple of muffled shots sounded. Obviously, Brian had his hands full.

"Let's plan the wedding later," I advised, fumbling with her ropes until I finally got one knot loose. "Right now, I suggest we get out of here."

"How did you get away?"

"Your friendly, neighborhood British commando."

We were out in the hallway. "There's no time for explanations now."

I shoved Karen down the hall. "Head to the door down to the left. Brian's Land Rover is parked by the pool."

I glanced over my shoulder and saw a pistol flare in quarter-light, and something burned in my shoulder. But I knew it was just the original hole, not a new one.

Swiveling back around, I ran straight forward, and right into Karen's back.

"Which door, Duffy? There's three or four of them!"

I was at a total loss, until an arm caught me around the waist. I rounded a fist on my new enemy, but a firm hand caught and held it in midair with a grunt. "You'd get lost in a one-room house, mate," I heard Brian whisper. "This way."

He shoved me and Karen through a dry-rotted door and into the desert night. "Where's Marina?" I asked.

"Dead."

"What?"

"Dead," Brian repeated. "We'll sort it all out in the Rover. I left your friends tied up back in the room."

We crammed into the Rover, and Brian threw it into gear and slammed his foot on the accelerator just as two of L. Bruce's thugs came around the corner of the pool. "We are pretty nearly fucked," Brian said, one eye pinned on the rearview.

"Would somebody tell me something?"

"Sorry, Karen, but your boy Brucie was running a high-class whorehouse for the dip crowd. Unfortunately, Marina was one of his bimbos. "

"Not anymore," Brian said. "They must have shot her up with something. It would seem that they flunked out of medical school. She was gone when I got there."

Nobody said anything for a second. Brian negotiated the rock-strewn road headed for the distant gate and the Fahaheel Expressway beyond.

"Just as well," I finally croaked. "Since she'd just watched her father blow his own brains out." Poor old Serge. No more wodka. No more whores. I already missed him.

"Mates," Brian said into the gap. "We've got a little problem, a red Jeep Cherokee just pulled away from the palace. Where do we go?"

"Only one place," Karen said.

"Yeah? Where's that? The Red Cross?"

"The U.S. Embassy."

Checking the rearview, I saw the red Cherokee bouncing along behind us. And while I watched, its rear wheel slipped into a rut and jarred to a halt, but in a second it was back on our tail. After six decades and several wars, we'd finally find out which was better, the Land Rover or the Jeep. "Punch it now, Brian. He'll kick four-wheel drive any second. We need a break."

"I'll give us a break, mate," he said. I slammed against the door while the Rover folded into a ninety-degree turn.

"Uh, Brian. The road's back there."

"This is faster. The embassy's just a half a mile across here."

"Uh, Brian. That sign says 'Danger. Land mines.'"

"Quit your moanin'. They're labeled." He pointed out the window.

Sure enough. A jillion little red flags flapped in the breeze, nearly covering the stretch of desert between us and the embassy. "That's well and good, but— "

"Don't interrupt," he snapped. "I'm concentrating."

"But, Brian, there's no goddamned road!"

"I have good reflexes," and he spun the wheel suddenly, sliding neatly around one of the flags. "See?"

I glanced back and saw the Cherokee hesitate at the edge of the minefield for a second before plunging in behind us.

"Are they back there?" Brian asked.

"Yes, and the Cherokee's gaining ground and they've got a back-up." I craned my head around to catch a better glimpse of the second vehicle—an Isuzu Trooper.

"Sorry, mate, but if I drive any faster we could end up knocking on St. Pete's door sooner rather than later. Besides, we've almost made it."

I saw that he was right. Only a hundred yards to go. A hundred yards filled with land mines, but a hundred yards is more comforting than three hundred.

And then the desert just lit up. A bright, orange glow blossomed behind us, followed almost immediately by a muffled explosion and then another and another and . . . .

"Poor bastards," I said as the Jeep flipped end over end, striking yet another mine every time it touched ground, each new explosion lighting up the sky with more fireworks. Then, after one final assist, the Jeep exploded in midair in a blaze of fire and an earsplitting roar.

"Oh, shit!" Brian spun around and I watched his eyes double in size, like two big silver dollars.

We were almost through the field, but that wasn't what had Brian speechless. It was this big, monster sand dune straight in front of us, and we were moving far too fast and were far too close to avoid it.

"Got your seat belt on?" I asked Karen.

"No," she answered, still staring at the fiery scene behind us. "But the Jeep accomplished one thing."

"What's that?" I was remarkably relaxed.

"It blew a pretty good-sized hole for the Isuzu to drive through, and they're gaining."

"Not for long," Brian answered.

With a lurch and a bump, the Land Rover was airborne.

CHAPTER
TWENTY-ONE

Time moved pretty slowly then. We sailed off the dune and realized almost immediately that Brian had been right. The U.S. Embassy really was only about a half mile away if you drove across the minefield. I deduced this from the surprised expressions on the security guards as we flew over the embassy wall, headed, it looked like, for the tennis courts. I waved at them as we passed. One of them gave a half-hearted response.

And there you have it. I checked our projected landing site, saw that it was about two seconds away, and closed my eyes in preparation for our imminent crash landing. Unfortunately, on this airline, I seemed to be the only one worried about my seat belt.

Time returned to normal at the exact moment that the headlights of the Land Rover plowed into the tennis court. My head started bouncing off the dashboard, opening a cut that sent a stream of blood into my eyes. Something slammed into the back of my seat, something that I hoped wasn't Karen.

Somebody stirred beside me, and I glanced over to see Brian lifting his head off the steering wheel, a cut like mine above his eye.

"Her Majesty's SAS, mate," Brian reminded me with a grin. "I can fly a bloody helo if I have to."

About that time, the U.S. Marines caught up with us, advancing carefully, M-16s pointed in our direction. I realized that Karen wasn't talking. She was slumped against the back of my seat, out cold. The hole in my shoulder had started oozing again. "Doesn't look like she's bleeding," I ventured.

"But we've got a squad of marines cocking and locking their weapons in our direction," Brian said. "We're both going to raise our hands. Sooner or later, they'll see the dip tags on this Rover."

A fresh-faced marine appeared in my side window about then, waving the business end of an M-16.

"Sir, keep your hands in the air and step away from the vehicle!"

I put my shoulder—my good shoulder—into the door, and it didn't budge, not even a millimeter. The marine gestured impatiently.

"Bloody, sodding door," Brian muttered. Apparently, he was having the same trouble.

"Sir, step away from the vehicle!"

As the soldier jerked on the door, Brian turned to me. "Let me do all the talking."

"Lend a hand, mate!" Brian shouted at the marine, and with a screech, a scratch, and a groan, the driver's side door finally opened.

"Step away from the vehicle, sir."

"Get your bloody weapon out of my face, son, before I make you eat it."

The marine blinked. But he let the barrel droop just a bit.

"That's a good lad. I'm Captain Brian O'Neill of Her Majesty's Armed Forces. I've got an injured American diplomat in here. She needs immediate attention."

To the kid's credit, he poked his head through the door, took a good, long look at Karen and backed out in a hurry.

"He's right! It's Karen Solomon, and the other one is that guy she was with at our last party! Looks like he took a bullet in the shoulder. Somebody go get the DCM and call Clarice!"

"Lads!" Brian reminded them.

And they snapped to, carrying first Karen and then Brian and me out of the Rover. I discovered that my right leg didn't seem to want to work; they turned me loose and I fell flat on my face. The trickle down my right shoulder wasn't clotting.

"You look like hell, Duffy," Karen said as her eyes fluttered open.

"You're no prize yourself, little darlin'." Not really sure whether I should joke at a time like that, but it was good to see her conscious and cutting.

Before I could reach over to her, a voice as familiar as the high school principal's sounded. "Okay! Back off, marines!" And I knew without turning to look that L. Bruce had not been in the red Cherokee.

"Hey, Brian?" He was lying on the other side of Karen, a corpsman working on the cut across his brow.

"Yeah, mate?"

"You don't have any spare hand grenades, do you?"

"Quiet, you morons!" L. Bruce had spoken.

God, if I looked half as bad as he did, well, close the casket door and plant me. One of his eyes was swollen shut and his shirt was torn half off. My shoulder hurt like a son of a bitch, but I couldn't resist.

"Bad day at the office, Brucie?"

"Shut up!" L. Bruce shouted again. "Arrest all three of them!"

The marines looked at us, then at Dalrymple, and then at each other. But nobody moved. I saw Frank skulking in the background.

"Arrest them, you cretins!"

"On what charge, sir? I mean, that's Karen Solomon."

"I don't care if she's the goddamned Pope! Arrest her for treason!"

This was the place where Karen was supposed to pull our chestnuts out of the fire. Unfortunately, other than those first couple of sentences, she had remained comatose.

"Marine," L. Bruce said, turning to the closest peachfuzz cheek. "Either arrest these three or you'll finish your tour in Leavenworth."

The kid blushed. Then, he turned to another soldier and said, "Go get the handcuffs."

With our fate decided, I looked around for Frank.

"This must be gratifying for you, Brucie," I said. "I'm beat all to hell. Karen's probably got a concussion. Brian's, well, Brian may actually kill you before this over. And you're standing there grinning like you've saved the world from annihilation." What the hell! If we were totally screwed, this was it anyway. But, even as I spoke, I was still trying to figure a way out of all this. "You need to get some perspective. You're not Jack Ryan, and we're not about to destroy the world."

"I don't suppose it occurred to you, mate," Brian began through gritted teeth, "that I have diplomatic immunity."

"Yeah," L. Bruce admitted. "Marine, put these three in my Isuzu."

The marine, after hearing that exchange, said. "But we have detention rooms here, sir. I mean, it's not like they're going anywhere."

"Marine, consider yourself on report." L. Bruce turned to another one. "You! You're in charge."

"NO, GODDAMNIT! *I'M IN CHARGE!*"

L. Bruce's eyes grew as big as cow chips.

CHAPTER
TWENTY-TWO

I'd seen this guy before. Not like he was dressed now, in a silk bathrobe, hair in forty different directions, but I'd seen him. Something about the way Frank quickly slithered away made me realize that this was a good turn of events. L. Bruce must have thought the same thing, because he stiffened and frowned like he had gas.

"What the goddamned hell is going on here?" The loud-speaker voice modulated a little, and our new arrival pulled up short, shaking his head back and forth as he assessed the scene.

"Ambassador Barlow," L. Bruce began, and I detected just a hint of fear in his voice. So, this was the U.S. ambassador to Kuwait. "I can explain this."

The ambassador didn't answer L. Bruce immediately, just kept taking it all in. The smoking remains of a Land Rover protruded from the tennis court. His marine detachment held its weapons trained on three apparent prisoners, two of whom were bleeding and the third, unconscious it seemed, was one of his diplomats. The deputy chief of mission seemed to be choreographing the opera, and he didn't seem to be wearing very well at all with his superior.

"From what I can see, these two are beat to a bloody pulp. Karen Solomon's lying over there half dead. I've got a Rover with British Embassy plates plowing up my tennis court, and you've got the entire marine unit out here ready to go to war. The problem, Dalrymple, is that I don't know who the hell we're about to attack." The ambassador paused for a second and studied Brian. "Don't I know you, son?"

Brian managed a feeble salute. "Captain Brian O'Neill, Her Majesty's Armed Forces, seconded to the British Embassy in Kuwait, sir."

"And you?" He pointed at me.

"Ed Duffy, of the Volunteer State, seconded to the Patriot Missile Program."

"I'll be a possum-eating hillbilly! Dalrymple, if you can explain this, I swear to God, I'll retire and go back to coon hunting on Second Creek."

"Ambassador," L. Bruce began in his most condescending tone. "This is one of those situations in which you need to maintain plausible deniability."

"Dalrymple . . ." the ambassador began, his fists clenching until the knuckles turned a dangerous white. "I may have had to take this goddamned job to stay in the hunt, but I don't have to listen to your shit. You and your cloak and dagger capers." Barlow stopped again and grabbed a marine by the elbow. "Put that rifle away and get Solomon to the infirmary."

"With all due respect," L. Bruce interrupted. "I must insist that you not interfere here, sir. This is a situation involving national security, and I'm operating under a directive from the National Security Council."

"I doubt that, Brucie," a welcome voice interrupted. Harvey Hanks sidled up to the ambassador and shook his head at the carnage. "I told you to watch your ass, Duffy."

"Yeah, I know, Harvey. But I've never been very good at following orders." My eyesight was slipping and Harvey was getting a little fuzzy.

The ambassador turned to Harvey. "You know this guy?"

"Duffy and I are old friends; Brian and I are buddies, too," Harvey affirmed.

Brian smiled wanly.

"I told you, Duffy. Serpentine. Serpentine."

The ambassador shook his head in disbelief. "I'm the keeper of a goddamned insane asylum. Duffy—is that your name? Can you walk?"

I tested my leg again and it held. I nodded. No way was I going to miss this show; the shoulder be damned.

The ambassador jerked his head at Hanks and L. Bruce. "Conference room. Now!"

And, with a little help from the marines, we headed into the inner courtyard and to the conference room I was coming to know so well. One of the marines helped me into a chair, and I closed my eyes as the rest shuffled into the room. It had been a truly long day. With my eyes closed, I could almost forget everything—Kirby, Serge, Marina, the ubiquitous Frank. Yeah, it all disappeared into a haze of purple morphine. Or was it a purple haze of morphine?

"It's like this, Ambassador," I managed to slur in his direction. "Your deputy, L. Bruce Dalrymple, was running a whorehouse to compromise foreign diplomats. A friend of mine"—and I winced as I realized I was classing Kirby Benson as my friend—"stumbled onto it, so Bruce and Frank had him killed. They were going to kill us too, but Brian here stormed the place and got us out." My explanation was just short of coherent.

"He's a goddamned English teacher!" an exasperated L. Bruce shouted.

"Humph," Barlow grunted and threw me a sour look. "Where are you from anyway? That accent sounds too damned familiar."

And that's when I remembered him. A former senator turned character actor turned, it appeared, diplomat. "You're the guy who was with Clint East—"

"A long time ago. Now, quit stomping around and get to the point."

I shrugged. "I got mixed up in it because Sergei Malenkov—"

"The Russian consul?" Barlow interrupted.

"That's the one. See, Serge's dead." That fuzzy haze that usually precedes unconsciousness started encroaching again, and I shook my head. Poor Serge, poor Marina, caught in a scam that would make James Bond blush. "If you'd hold your questions to the end, I could get through this without passing out. Maybe."

Barlow's head snapped back, and after a second he nodded.

"One thing led to another and before I knew it, I was watching Brucie's boys dragging my roommate into the same whorehouse that I'd just seen Serge's daughter go into."

"Then . . . the next day . . . when I found old Kirby floating . . . face down . . . in the Gulf, well," I shook my head as the morphine haze covered the room, "you can imagine my surprise."

"Ambassador," L. Bruce began. "How long do we have to sit here and listen to the rantings of this treasonous scoundrel?"

"Awwh," came a new voice from the door. "I think this is long enough. I can fill in anything else the ambassador needs to know."

If I'd been confused before, I was over the edge by then. The best I could manage was a weak, "Hey, Fitzy," and then pain, fatigue, and loss of blood won, and I passed right on out.

CHAPTER
TWENTY-THREE

And, so, I found myself back at the Kuwait International Airport, now completely oblivious to Arabs with cell phones pressed to their ears and pagers beeping ominously on their hips. This time, though, the effervescent Fitzy was joined by my old friend, Harvey Hanks of the Central Intelligence Agency, to see me off. Somehow, that made all the sense in the world. We unloaded my bags and stacked them on the sidewalk where they were immediately surrounded by the same buzzing Pakistani skycaps.

"What'll happen now?" I asked.

Harvey grinned. "L. Bruce will have to find another line of work, I'm afraid. Maybe even in one of those white-collar country clubs they call prisons. It all depends."

"On what?" Seemed pretty cut-and-dried to me.

"On all those powers-that-be, Duffy," Fitzy said. "Sometimes they don't like to air their dirty laundry in front of the world."

Fitzy, it turned out, was one of Harvey's boys, assigned to keep an eye on Frank. We had shut down the English language component of the Patriot project and all the teachers were scattered to the four winds. Barlow kept me in-country long enough to recover and to probe for everything I knew about L. Bruce's operation. Karen had been medevaced to Frankfurt, Germany, and then to Washington. Brian received a commendation, a reprimand, and a notice of early retirement, in that order. Kirby's body had been flown back to the states where, I understood, his son awaited.

"What about Frank?"

"Frank's history too," Fitzy said. "You see, Duffy, you just can't go around indiscriminately killing American citizens. It's a no-win proposition."

"How's that? I didn't think you guys had any qualms about killing if it accomplished the mission."

"There's always somebody like you out there to yank us up by the short hairs," Harvey said, dropping the used-car salesman patter.

"So, Fitz, were you really a Peace Corps volunteer?"

The pair of them looked shocked. "Absolutely not, Duffy," Harvey answered. "It's against the law for the Company to recruit former PCVs. But it's not against the law to masquerade as a former PCV. It was a great cover. Frank never suspected Fitzy for a minute."

"Truth is, Duffy," Fitzy chimed in, "Frank can't find his ass with both hands in the classroom *or* in covert operations."

"You've got a gift, Duffy," Harvey began. "People trust you. They take one look at you and immediately trust you. They spill out their whole life for you. And you've got guts. Shit, I've got fully trained officers that would mess their pants in your situation. Think about it. The Company could use somebody like you. *I* could use you out here. It's a war, Duffy. We're on the front lines."

"I thought America was at peace."

"America is at peace, Duffy," Harvey admonished, "because the CIA is at war."

I patted him on the shoulder. You couldn't help but like Harvey. "No thanks, bud. I've had all the adventure I can stand for one lifetime. Besides, I keep thinking about poor old Kirby floating in the Gulf. And Serge with half his head blown off. And Marina; she was just a kid."

"Hey, we didn't kill them," Fitzy reminded me.

"I know, but Brucie did. And for what? A whorehouse. And Kirby thought he was onto the story of a lifetime."

"Yeah, ummh, well." Suddenly Harvey was at a loss for words. He and Fitzy shuffled their feet and looked the other way.

"What?" Then, the truth hit me. "Don't tell me. Jesus H. Christ! Don't tell me that little fuzzball *was* onto something."

A weak little grin spread across Harvey's face. "Jeez, Duffy, I could go to jail for this, but, hell, you deserve to know. Old Kirby was right on the money. By our best estimates, Gulf War Syndrome was caused when Iraqi bombs took out a secret Kuwaiti chemical weapons plant. The resulting fallout contaminated an area about the size of Rhode Island."

"And we've been covering for the Kuwaitis all these years?"

"Yeah, I know, Duff. It sounds like a raw deal, but we have to be here. With all these rogues and madmen, we've got to have a substantial foothold in the region. The Kuwaitis have given us that."

"So, let me get this straight. If Bruce hadn't killed Kirby, you would have?"

"Naw," Fitzy answered. "Nobody would have believed him. He'd be like Jim Garrison and the JFK assassination conspiracy. He'd never have had any conclusive proof. Maybe someday Oliver Stone would have done a movie about him, but it would still just be a crackpot theory."

That was something I knew I couldn't handle. I don't know what it was—maybe it was all the wear and tear on my body, maybe it was the revelation that Kirby wasn't the big idiot everyone thought, but events had taken on a telescopic perspective, like I was looking at the world through a long tunnel.

"Take care of yourself, Duffy. I'm pretty sure I'll be seeing you again."

"Don't say that, Harvey. Even in jest."

Fitzy stuck his hand out. "You sure you won't change your mind? We could do a lot of damage, Duff."

"Thanks, but I'm damaged enough as it is. You're a good guy, Fitzy. I'm gonna miss you."

Those blue eyes twinkled, and then the passport control booths swallowed me up and shunted me into a freefall toward Tennessee. And when the flight attendant came by as we lifted off, I waved goodbye to the refinery fires, the lights of Salmiya, and the ghosts of my friends, and I ordered a double whiskey.

EPILOGUE

Kuwait is another planet, and I've returned to the land of fried chicken, iced tea, and honeysuckle in bloom. I came home to be what I always should have been, a teacher of literature, not a teacher of English. I filed for bankruptcy and started anew at age forty.

Brian's a financial planner in London now, happily it seems. Harvey sends me occasional cards and the most recent informed me that Frank, at last contact, was serving as an advisor to some Third-World dictator, teaching classes in the rubber-hose school of interrogation. He avoided prison, unlike L. Bruce, who just finished an eighteen-month stay at Eglin Air Force Base.

Fitzy resigned from the CIA and was elected to Teddy Kennedy's old seat in Boston. He parlayed his Boston blue-collar background into some kind of populist, second Camelot thing and won in a landslide. Nobody brought up his CIA background. I guess voters were looking for a Kennedy-free alternative. They could have done worse.

Karen? We have plans to marry. When? Oh, someday. Someday when her love of travel becomes as sated as mine.

And Kuwait? It's still there, holding its own in the menacing shadow of Saddam Hussein.

Me, I stay in the classroom and away from patriots. You see, the trouble with patriots is that they're all willing to die for the cause, even when they have no clue what the cause looks like.